FireDance

Joseph Padgal

FireDance

ISBN: 978-1-60920-002-2
Printed in the United States of America
©2010 by Joseph Padgal
All rights reserved

Cover and interior design by Isaac Publishing, Inc.

Library of Congress Cataloging-in-Publication Data

IPI
Isaac Publishing, Inc.
P.O. 342
Three Rivers, MI 49093
www.isaacpublishing.com

No part of this book may be reproduced or transmitted in any form or by any means, electronic or mechanical—including photocopying, recording, or by any information storage and retrieval system—without permission in writing from the publisher, except as provided by United States of America copyright law.

Please direct your inquiries to admin@isaacpublishing.com

FireDance

Joseph Padgal

IPI Isaac Publishing
P.O. Box 342 Three Rivers, MI 49093
888.273.4JOY
www.isaacpublishing.com

Foreword

As a professional Christian counselor, author and ordained pastor, I realize that forgiveness is a very important issue. In my daily contact with clients, I cannot emphasize it more. Mr. Padgal has written a good book about forgiveness and how it applies to sexual abuse. The characters he portrays are just like you and me, facing crisis, dealing with the pain of hurtful memories and struggling with forgiving the people that caused them. I believe God instituted forgiveness not just for the victim but for the perpetrator as well. Forgiving the person who hurt you says, "I give up my right to hold them accountable for what they did to me." This is a tough call for the victim, especially in a society that screams, "I want justice for myself and punishment for my offender!" Mr. Padgal brings in generational issues as a basis for the abuse he writes about. Nobody on the face of this earth can escape that. What our ancestors said in the form of curses and blessings or the hurts and abuses they suffered will follow us through time like our shadow on a sunny day. Only through Christ can they be broken. I recommend this book for anyone. We all need to forgive...seventy times seven.

Pastor Craig S. Mattheson
Author of Sex, Romance, Marriage & Relationships

Disclaimer

Though loosely derived from personal experiences, this book is a work of fiction. Any names or details that may be similar to or pertain to any person, living or dead, or specific place or circumstance have been changed to disguise and protect the innocent. Please be advised that the material presented is sensitive, pertains to sexual abuse, and may cause emotional responses for which the author is not responsible.

FIREDANCE ◆ 8

An Everyday Flight

"Forgiveness is God's invention for coming to terms with a world in which, despite their best intentions, people are unfair to each other and hurt each other deeply. He began by forgiving us. And he invites us all to forgive each other."

Lewis B. Smedes, *Forgive & Forget:
Healing the Hurts We Don't Deserve*

Waves softly lapped the shores of the Great Lake island as the late afternoon sun warmed its sandy beaches. Soft to moderate winds blew the patches of weeds growing along the lakeshore back and forth like an old man rubbing his head to see how much hair he had left. Along the shore, two children were playing tag with the waves as a large white gull dove into the water to snare a fish. High above, a plane piloted by Michael Jacobson made its way along the west side of Baker's Island, fifteen hundred feet above County Road Seventeen. To Michael, flying his 1958 Beechcraft Travel Air came as naturally as his next breath. It was a sturdy workhorse of a plane that he faithfully serviced and maintained.

Every day, Michael followed County Road Seventeen home as closely as a motorist's finger would trace the same road on a road map. Michael glanced out the side window of the planes cabin at his left engine. The amber gold light from the setting sun reflected off the waves on the lake. This reflected light animated the flames painted on the engine cover, giving Michael the illusion that they were dancing. He smiled, knowing that this natural everyday splendor gave him the name for his plane. Eventually County Road Seventeen turned inland in a slow, lazy angle heading toward the busy little town of Crandon, Michigan. This was Michael's cue to start his landing approach on the east-to-west runway that sat not too far off the north side of his home.

 Soon the plane's wheels touched down on the runway. Michael slowed the aircraft down, turning it toward the back of the old hangar built by his father. Michael drove his plane through the opened rear entrance and stopped it. Turning off its motors, he grabbed his lunch box, climbed out of the aircraft, and closed the cabin door.

He set his lunch box down on one wing and stood with his arms folded watching his four-year-old daughter, Sarah, and Riley, their Labrador retriever. Sarah sat in her two-wheeled pull cart that was harnessed to Riley, who followed Teaser, their tabby cat. Suddenly Teaser took off, zigzagging across the yard in hot pursuit of a butterfly. Riley snorted, stopping to mark his territory. Sarah watched him for a while, then picked up the reins and slapped them across his back. Riley finished what he was doing, looked back at her, and snorted again. Then he began ambling along, hardly motivated to do anything more strenuous. Michael stood watching all this with a big smile on his face, realizing he wouldn't trade moments like these for all the gold in the world.

Michael picked up his lunch box off the wing. He walked out of the hangar and over to the back door of their 1850s brick colonial-style home that he had inherited from his father. He opened the back door and walked over to his wife, Cindy, who was making a big pot of his favorite stew on the stove. Michael kissed her on her neck. As she turned around, she smiled at him. "Here, try some of this and tell me if I've put in the right amount of spices." Cindy put a wooden spoon heaped with stew into Michael's mouth. Savoring it, he responded in an almost proper English accent. "My dear, you have succeeded in making yet another culinary masterpiece." She smiled, turned, and washed off the spoon in the sink, sticking it back into the pot of stew on the stove.

Cindy focused her eyes on him. "Can you tell me why I couldn't get you on the two-way radio today?" Michael looked at her like a child caught with his hands in the cookie jar. "Cindy, I'm sorry. I forgot to turn mine on." Cindy made a face. "What if there was an emergency down here and I had to call you? Would I have to shoot something up in the air at you to get your attention? If I had, I might have accidently shot you down. Not because I was a bad shot, but because I'd be that mad at you." Then Cindy laughed with an impish grin on her face. "That would have gotten your attention!" She sighed and frowned. "I'm sorry, that's not funny. Please forgive me." Michael looked at her. "No, you're right; I should have had it on." Suddenly a distant stare filled his eyes. Cindy knew this stare. It meant that he was going to blurt out something totally unrelated to what they were talking about. Michael looked at his wife. "Cindy, I had a bad dream about my parents' old bedroom last night. I don't know what it meant, but I woke up sick to my stomach." Cindy looked at him for a moment, wondering what inspired such a dream. She knew he never talked about his parents, let alone their bedroom. Cindy watched him as he walked out of the kitchen. She sighed, turned back to the stove, and began to stir the stew she had just made.

During supper, Abby, their eleven-year-old, looked at her dad. "Hey, Dad, where were you today? I couldn't get you on your radio to tell you my good news. I got an A-plus in math today. Aren't you proud of me?" Michael was embarrassed. He looked at Cindy for moral support. Cindy shrugged her shoulders. "Don't look at me; I didn't tell her to say that." Michael smiled, looking at his daughter. "Sweetheart, I'm VERY proud of you for getting the A-plus. Please call me anytime you want to talk on the radio." Abby smiled, giving her dad a big hug. Later after all the dishes were washed and put away, the family took their turns in the bathroom and went to bed. Soon after they were asleep, the darkness crept in.

The Darkness

"The rule is: we cannot really forgive ourselves unless we look at the failure in our past and call it by its right name."

Lewis B. Smedes, Forgive & Forget:
Healing the Hurts We Don't Deserve

At midnight that same night, a severe thunderstorm blew out of the northwest. It swept down on the island, toppling trees, taking down power lines, and spreading debris all over the island. When the storm hit the Jacobson homestead, the mercury lights in the yard and the lights in the house flickered, then went out, plunging everything into total blackness. Inside the house, a mysterious dark part of Michaels past crept down the hallway toward the bedroom where he and his wife were sleeping. Inside Michael's sleeping mind, images of people he knew long ago were reaching out and grabbing at him. Others were screaming his name. Suddenly, he felt a hauntingly strange but familiar pain in his body.

Outside, a brilliant flash of lightning was followed by a huge crash of thunder, shook the house. Suddenly Michael sat straight up in bed and screamed. Michael jumped out of bed, still yelling. "I've got to run to the mill!"

Cindy jerked awake, jumped out of bed, and tackled Michael, causing him to fall backward onto the floor with her on top of him. "MICHAEL! It's a bad dream! You're okay! You're okay!"

Hearing her voice, Michael stopped struggling and looked up at her. Between flashes of lightning she saw a look on his face that she had never seen before--that of a hurt and frightened child. Michael was soaked in his own sweat, and his heart felt like it was beating out of his chest. Cindy got off of him, struggling to get him propped up in a sitting position against one of the walls near the foot of the bed. She was breathing hard. "Stay here… I'm going to check on the girls." Michael grabbed her arm. "Don't leave me, Grace!" Cindy stopped and looked at him in the darkness. Why did he call her his sister's name? Suddenly fear and confusion gripped her like a pair of unseen hands around her throat. It didn't help that the wind was howling around the old house or than there were strange noises she had never heard before.

Bang! The screen door to the kitchen suddenly flew open, slamming against the house. Cindy jumped, her heart pounding in her chest. She broke into a cold sweat. She looked down at Michael sitting against the bedroom wall. "Michael, I'll be gone just a minute, okay?"

Michael didn't say a word. He let go of her arm, sitting there motionless. Cindy fumbled around in the darkness, finding the flashlight that she kept in her night stand. Turning it on, she held it on Michael for a moment, then walked out of the bedroom and down the hall. Shining the light down the hallway, she heard Sarah crying. The first room after the upstairs landing was Abby's. Cindy opened her door and called out. "Abby! Do you want to come to our bedroom?" Abby was already up and suddenly appeared out of the darkness. Cindy jumped, almost dropping her flashlight. "ABBY! You scared me half to death!"

"I'm sorry, Mom. Yes, I do want to be with you and Dad. I've been hearing creepy noises coming from the bedroom next to me." Cindy shivered and looked at her. "That was your grandparents' old bedroom. Oh, it doesn't matter now. Just put on your bathrobe and we'll get your sister!"

Together they left Abby's bedroom walking down the hall to Sarah's bedroom. As they opened her door, a sudden blast of wind screeched through an open window in the opposite bedroom. Its door suddenly flew open! Cindy and Abby jumped and screamed!

Cindy had to shout over the noise the wind was making. "Let's get Sarah!" Cindy opened Sarah's bedroom door, went in, and picked Sarah up out of her bed. Sarah wrapped her arms around her mother. Cindy talked softly to her. "It's okay, it's okay, Sarah."

With the wind howling and moaning at them from the old bedroom, they started to walk down the darkened hallway. When they reached the upstairs landing, their imaginations had gotten the best of them. The strange shadows that the lightning was bringing to life were following and reaching out for them with their dark, spidery arms.

They started running.

They ran into Cindy and Michael's bedroom, slamming the door behind them. They ran over to the bed and sat on it, holding on to each other. Soon after that, the lights came back on. Cindy exhaled. "Thank you God!"

A short while later the bedroom door opened and Michael walked in, wiping his damp hair with a towel. Cindy sat there staring at him. Michael looked back at her. "Are you okay?"

Cindy didn't say anything as she sat Sarah down and got off the bed. She walked over to Michael and wrapped her arms around his waist. "Please hold me and tell me that you're okay."

Michael put his arms around her and kissed her. "Of course I am. It's just a plain old thunderstorm, that's all."

Cindy looked up at his face. "Don't you remember anything that just happened?"

Michael looked at her. "I found myself propped up against the bedroom wall half soaked in my own sweat. I thought that was strange so I got up, found my flashlight and walked across the hall into the bathroom. I was going to take a shower when I remembered that the electricity was off to the well pump. So I sat down on the edge of the tub for a while and waited. About fifteen minutes later the lights came on and I took one. Now what is it that I am supposed to remember?"

Cindy looked back at their daughters sitting on the bed and sighed. "I'll tell you tomorrow." Together they walked over to their bed and climbed in with the girls between them. Cindy looked at

Abby next to her. "Do you want to sleep with the light on?" Abby smiled. "No, like Dad said, it's just a plain old thunderstorm."

The Voices From The Closet

"...Forgiving is not having to understand. Understanding may come later, in fragments, an insight here and a glimpse there, after forgiving."

Lewis B. Smedes, Forgive & Forget:
Healing the Hurts We Don't Deserve

Around seven that same morning, Michael and Cindy woke up and unpeeled themselves from around their sleeping daughters. Leaving them in their bed, Michael and Cindy put on their bathrobes and walked down the hallway, slowly descending the back stairs that led to the kitchen. Cindy turned the lights on and walked over to the stove, turning on one of the burners to heat water in the teakettle.

Michael walked over to the kitchen window facing the hangar. "I can't believe it. You should see all the tree limbs that the storm took down last night, Cindy."

Cindy was half listening to him. She was still thinking about the events that happened during the storm. She turned away from the stove and looked at him. "I don't care about the tree limbs! I want to know what happened with you last night."

Michael turned away from the window and looked at her. "I don't know what you're talking about."

Cindy stared at him, pouring some hot water into two mugs and adding a tea bag to each. "Okay, let's sit over here and I'll tell you." Michael turned slowly, walking over to the bench in the nook. Cindy picked up the mugs and set them on the table. Then she sat down next to Michael. She continued to stare at him as she took a spoon and wrung out the tea bags.

Michael didn't show any concern as he shrugged his shoulders. "So what happened besides a big storm?" Stirring her tea, she looked at him.

"During the storm there was an unusually loud crash of thunder that shook the house. Usually you sleep right through a storm and so do I, but not this one. You jumped out of bed soaked in sweat, screaming, 'I've got to run to the mill!' You had a frightened, hurt look on your face, like a child who had just been beaten. I've never seen you with a look like that. When I said I had to go and check on the girls, you said, 'Please don't leave me alone, Grace!' You called me by your sister's name. Why did you do that?"

Michael looked around the kitchen, then back at her. "Cindy, I really don't know why I acted that way. I do remember sitting against the bedroom wall wondering how I got there. I heard you talking to Abby down the hall and heard Sarah crying. I felt stupid sitting there, so I got up and went into the bathroom to take a shower. The rest you know." He looked away, then back at her.

"Okay," he continued, "maybe this will help. About two days ago I was sorting through the closet in the den, when I came across my dad's old reel- to-reel tape recorder. I noticed there was a tape on it marked 'Michael's Tenth Birthday.' I got curious, plugged it in, and turned it on. I knew my dad recorded our birthdays and holidays when my sister and I were kids. I thought it might be interesting to listen to. All I heard was me and my sister and a few friends laughing and making all kinds of noises, along with the sound of tearing paper. I also heard the voices of my uncle Dick and aunt Ruth and my mom and dad. I didn't think that anything was unusual until my dad said something to me on the tape.

"All of a sudden I turned off the recorder, unplugged it, and stuffed it as far back in the closet as I could. I can't remember what my dad said, but whatever it was made me nauseous. Does that help?"

Cindy sat there looking at him, trying to mentally digest what Michael had said. Finally she spoke. "Michael, I don't know. But if you don't mind I'd like to talk to Jenny about this."

Michael shrugged his shoulders again. "I don't mind. Jenny's an old college friend of mine and a good counselor. Maybe she can shed some light on it. Oh, by the way, my sister called yesterday and left her phone number. She said she wanted to get together with you and talk about my family."

Cindy had a puzzled look on her face. "That's

strange. After all these years she only wants to talk with me. What about you? Don't you matter?"

Michael agreed. "I'd like to see Grace too, but she said she only wanted to talk to you. I guess I'll have to wait."

Cindy sighed. "Where did you put her phone number?"

Michael pointed to the notepad that hung on a string near the wall phone. He turned toward her on the bench. "Frank Clayton called from the airport saying the storm took down a lot of trees and damaged a number of buildings. He said they closed the airport for a couple of days. Since I can't fly into town, I thought I'd clean up all the limbs around the house."

Cindy smiled. "Good! It'll be nice to have you here on the ground instead of in the air all the time."

Early the next morning, Cindy woke up to the sound of a chain saw. She sat up in bed and yawned, realizing that Michael had gotten up earlier and started cutting up fallen tree limbs. Cindy got out of bed, stretched, and put on her bathrobe. She walked out of the bedroom into the bathroom turning on the water in the shower. Suddenly she turned it off and walked out of the bathroom, down the hall to the last bedroom on the right. The door was locked, so she took the key off the hook above the door and unlocked it. Cindy slowly turned the door handle, opening the squeaky door. Reaching around the door frame, she turned on the light switch. Cobwebs covering the light fixture on the ceiling, cast eerie shadows on drop cloths covering the old furniture in the room.

Strong breezes were blowing through an opened window, causing the drop cloths to flap and an old rocking chair to move. Cindy watched the old chair rocking back and forth in the breeze until it suddenly stopped moving. She thought she saw something out of the corner of her eye, moving toward her from that direction. Cindy flinched and spoke out loud. "Who's there?" The breezes had caused an old lace curtain to billow out across the old chair. Sighing, she walked over to the window, closing and latching it. Then she turned, walking straight out of the room, turning off the light and locking the door behind her. Cindy exhaled as she replaced the key on its hook. So much for the creepy noises that Abby had heard!

Cindy walked back down the hallway into the bathroom. She shivered again. That room gave her the strangest feeling in the pit of her stomach. Later when she had finished up in the bathroom and gotten dressed, she woke up the girls, making sure they washed up and got dressed for the day.

At breakfast Abby and Sarah sat at the table in the kitchen nook across from Cindy. She looked at Abby. "Did you know that someone closed and locked the door to the room across from Sarah's last night?" Cindy looked at Sarah, who had oatmeal on most of the lower half of her face, then back at Abby. Abby sighed. "Yes, and I know who did it too."

Cindy looked at her, wiping oatmeal off Sarah's face with a paper towel. "Go on, I'm listening."

Abby explained, "When the lights went out, I

got up and walked over to my bedroom door and opened it. I looked out and there was Dad unlocking the door to that creepy old bedroom. I said, 'Hi, Dad.' But he didn't say anything to me. He walked in and I heard him open a window. Then he came out, leaving the door open a little, and walked back down the hallway into your bedroom."

"Then I heard him scream. Later you came down the hall into my room and we got Sarah. Dad did something else strange after we were all sleeping. I had to go to the bathroom. As I was crossing the hall, I saw him go down the hallway and lock the door to that old bedroom. After that, he came back to your room.

"Both times Dad's eyes were wide open. He didn't talk to me or even see me. Why was Dad acting like that?"

Cindy was about to respond when she looked out the kitchen window. "Abby, I think your school bus is here." Abby had just finished her breakfast. She washed and dried her hands, then hugged her mother goodbye. Cindy got up and walked out the back door, watching her daughter leave. When Abby climbed on the bus, Cindy walked back to the house and into the kitchen. Sarah sat in her chair with a spoon in one hand and the other inside her bowl, stuffing handfuls of dripping oatmeal into her mouth.

Suddenly Cindy stared at Sarah, pretending to look angry. Sarah looked up at her with her eyes widening and started to use her spoon. Cindy burst out laughing. "Caught you, didn't I?" Then she picked Sarah out of her chair with her spoon still in her hand, carrying her under one arm. "Just for that I'm going to wash your face in the sink and tickle you." Sarah laughed and squealed.

Outside Michael finished piling up the last of the fallen tree limbs. In the house Cindy had taken Sarah upstairs for her nap. As she came down the back stairway, she remembered what Michael said about Grace wanting to get together with her. She walked over to the wall phone and punched in some numbers.

"Hello? Jenny? I didn't wake you up, did I? Okay, good. Anyway, Michael got a call from his sister Grace just the other day. She wanted to get together with me and talk about Michael's family. No, she didn't want to talk to him. I was wondering if you could talk with her." Jenny agreed, mentioning that both of them should be at her office at ten the next morning.

Cindy hung up the phone, then looked out the window at Michael sitting on the picnic table, drinking from his water bottle. She picked up the pad that hung by the wall phone. Reading it, she punched in Grace's phone number on the handset. She waited, looking at the clock on the kitchen wall. "Hello, Grace, this is Cindy." After a short conversation, Grace agreed to meet Cindy at Jenny's office in Crandon.

As she hung up the phone, she looked out the kitchen window at Michael again. Turning around, she walked over to the refrigerator and pulled out some lunch meat to make sandwiches, along with vegetables for a salad. After she made lunch, she walked over to the kitchen door and opened it. "Michael, please come in and eat."

Michael put down the chain saw he was carrying. "Okay, sweetheart, I'll be right in and get cleaned up." During lunch Cindy told Michael that Grace would be meeting her the next morning in town at Jenny's office. Michael put down his fork and looked at her. "I can see this is turning into an all girl thing, but when you get back from town tomorrow, could you please fill me in on what you talked about?"

Cindy gave him a concerned look. "All I'm going to share is what happened the night of the storm. Some strange things happened that scared me. I don't mean the thunder and lightning or lights going out. I mean the way you reacted because of the storm. It scared me because I've never seen you like that!" Cindy sighed and kissed him. "Michael, whatever it is that you are going through, I'll be right beside you all through it."

Michael smiled. "Speaking of being right beside me, how about you and me snuggling up on the couch and watching a movie before Sarah wakes up and Abby comes home from school?"

Later after supper that evening, Cindy checked on Abby to see if she was doing her homework and gave Sarah her bath. When she came back to the kitchen, Cindy found Michael sitting in the kitchen nook working on his flight itinerary for the next day. She walked over to the table, sitting down in a chair across from him, resting her chin in her hands.

"I'm surprised that you're doing your itinerary. I thought the airport was closed because of the damage from the storm." Michael looked up at her. "I just got a call from Frank Clayton. He said it was open for business. Apparently most of the damage was in town, and from what he said the power company was expecting a lot of outages. They had crews right out in the middle of it, putting the wires back up almost as fast as they were going down. I guess that's why we got our power back so quickly." Michael looked back down at his itinerary and started writing.

Cindy cleared her throat. "So what are you going to do with the little girl once you pick her up at the airport?"

Michael looked up at her. "Have you been reading my flight itinerary again?"

Cindy smiled broadly. "Yes, for the past twenty years or so." Michael made a face at her. "Well! If you don't already know, I rigged up a cot in the back of the plane. I'll strap the little girl into the cot and fly her and her mother to the mainland where an ambulance will take them to a specialist."

Cindy smiled at him. "That's sweet of you to do that. But how did all this come about?"

Michael raised his eyebrows. "Well, Dave Tyler had a gallstone operation at the hospital and I had just come out of his room. I had just passed the nurses' station when I heard this woman crying from a nearby room. Curious, I walked over and knocked lightly on the door.

"I looked around the door and there sat this poor woman with tears streaming down her face. I cleared my throat and asked if there was anything

I could do to help her. She looked at me with those swollen, red eyes of hers and said all she needed was someone to talk to. Cindy, I just about cried. Sometimes I take it for granted that I have a wonderful wife and family to share my problems with, and here this poor woman didn't have anyone. I walked in and sat down beside her and introduced myself.

"I asked her if she had any relatives I could contact for her. She said that both her parents were dead. She was an only child so she didn't have any brothers or sisters. The only other relatives she had lived out of state and she didn't know them that well.

"Between sobs she told me that her husband had been killed in his car at a railroad crossing and that that his funeral was just last week. She said the insurance company was refusing to release the death benefit check because of a pending investigation of the accident.

"She went on to explain that her daughter had multiple sclerosis and needed a specialist on the mainland. She said that she didn't know how she was going to pay the hospital bills, because her husband had been the only one working and she didn't know if his health insurance would cover them now that he was gone.

"I sat there realizing how blessed my family and I were and how much this mother and her daughter needed a miracle. Then I got an idea. You know those CDs I cashed in and the World War II collection of my grandfather's that I sold?" Cindy smiled with tears in her eyes. "Well, the guy who bought it paid me thirty-five thousand dollars in cash. That's way too much cash to carry around, so I had our bank make money orders out of it. I wanted to keep the money, but I could see that she needed it more. I reached into my jacket, taking out the envelope with the money orders in it and gave it to her. She opened it up and looked inside. I told her, 'They're yours. All you need to do is put your name in as the payee because I have already signed them.'

"She sat there for almost five minutes trying to make sense of what had just happened. Then her hands began to shake, causing her to drop the envelope containing the money orders onto the floor. I was starting to pick it up for her when she looked at me with tears in her eyes, saying that she didn't know how to thank me enough for what I had done.

"I thought for a minute, then I told her she could thank me by letting me fly her daughter to the mainland free of charge. I told her that I had an old friend that worked in the state insurance commissioner's office. I told her I was sure that once my friend contacted her insurance company and talked with them, they would work out a solution to her problem."

Michael went on to explain that he exchanged contact information with the woman. She told him that she would talk to the doctors and let him know when he could fly them to the mainland. "When I got up to leave she gave me a hug, saying that maybe there was a God now that he had sent an angel to her.

"That's why I'm flying Marilyn and her daughter in my plane. I hope you're not mad at me for giving her all that money. I mean, she just lost her husband and…"

Cindy wrapped her arms around him. "No, I am not! Besides, she was right; you are an angel. That's why I married you, Michael Jacobson. You have a giving heart, and no matter how hard you try to keep it a secret, people are going to find out about it." Cindy was thankful that she had a husband that didn't hesitate to give so freely or care so unconditionally about other people.

Dark Family Secrets

"To forgive is to set a prisoner free and discover that the prisoner was you."
Philip Yancey - The Unnatural Act
(article, Christianity Today, April 8, 1991)

    The next morning the sun slowly rose over the nearby lake where the old mill sat, shining through the forest on the north side of the runway and into the kitchen windows. A gentle breeze was blowing through the back screen door, and the only noise was the rustling of the wind through the leaves of the trees. What a beautiful day for a flight!
    Michael went through his pre-flight check and looked over his itinerary, making a note of the cot in back. Satisfied that everything was okay, he stepped up onto the wing, opened the cabin door, and climbed in. He taxied his plane out of the hangar and onto the runway. Startled by the noise of the engines, a flock of birds took off in a swarm.
    Michael taxied the plane out to the runway. He eased its throttles forward. The plane rolled faster and faster until it lifted off the ground. Michael

cleared the trees on the southwest side of the runway, making his usual pass over the house where Cindy was. Hearing his plane fly overhead, she walked over to the back screen door and opened it. As usual, Michael wiggled the tail rudder of his plane from side to side, like he was waving at her. Cindy waved back at him. She blew him a kiss, then walked back into the kitchen. She glanced at the ancient regulator clock that hung on the kitchen wall. It was Saturday, and Cindy had called Janice Benson to come and watch the girls while she went into town to talk with Jenny.

Soon Janice drove up in her car, parking it near the carport. She got out, walked over to the back door, and knocked. Cindy opened the door for her, giving her some last minute suggestions, then walked over to the station wagon under the carport. Cindy drove out of their driveway onto County Road Seventeen, checking the house to make sure the windows were closed, because it looked like rain. Cindy had just passed Crandon's city limits sign when she turned onto Sycamore Street. A short while later she turned into the parking lot behind Jenny's office.

Jenny Peterson, the town's abuse counselor, had pulled into the parking lot earlier and gotten out of her car. As Cindy parked the station wagon, she noticed Jenny standing and talking to a neatly dressed woman who had parked her car next to Jenny's. Cindy got out of her vehicle and walked over to them. The woman turned and faced her. Cindy smiled and hugged her. "Grace, it's good to see you!"

Grace hugged Cindy back. "It's good to see you too."

Jenny interrupted them. "Ladies, I suggest we go to my office and talk, because it looks like it's going to rain any minute." Cindy broke Grace's embrace, looking over her shoulder to see if she left any windows open on the station wagon. All three of them made it inside the building when it started raining, lightning, and thundering.

Jenny smiled at Cindy and Grace. "Well, it looks like we have the place to ourselves today; Charlene, my secretary, is off, and I have no other appointments scheduled."

Jenny looked around the reception area. "Now let's see where Charlene stashes that great coffee she is always bragging about." Jenny pulled a bag from Charlene's desk. She walked over to the coffeemaker, measured some coffee from the bag into a paper filter, and placed it in its holder in the machine. As the hot liquid was starting to drip into the glass pot, she turned, looking at Grace. "How would you like yours?"

"Just put a little cream in mine." Jenny looked at Cindy. "I'd like the same, thanks." After all the women had gotten their coffee, they helped themselves to freshly baked muffins that Jenny had bought earlier.

All three women walked down a hallway into Jenny's office. Once inside the room, Jenny flipped on a light switch, motioning to some chairs arranged in a triangle, near a window on one side. Grace took the chair nearest to the window and Cindy sat down in one of the others. Before she sat down, Jenny walked over to her desk and retrieved her notebook. As she sat down, Jenny set a flashlight on the floor next to her. "I got this just in case the lights go out."

Then she cleared her throat. "Before we get started, I want you both to know that what is said in this office is kept confidential. Now which one of you ladies wants to go first?"

Cindy looked at Grace. "Do you mind if I start? What I have to share won't take too long and besides, you grew up with Michael so you probably will have more to talk about." Grace nodded. Jenny turned her attention to Cindy, flipping open her notebook with her pen poised to write.

Cindy took a deep breath and looked at Jenny, telling her all that had happened the night of the storm. After Cindy was finished, Jenny looked at the tears running down Grace's face and handed her a box of tissues. Grace thanked her, taking out some tissues and blowing her nose. Jenny looked at her. "Grace, do you want to risk getting in touch with the source of your pain?"

Grace answered, "Yes, I've been holding in too much hurt too long; it needs to come out." She took a deep breath. "Life at our home was wonderful when we were growing up. Our parents were the most loving, supportive parents any child could have. My brother was my best friend. We played with each other constantly. Our house was always filled with laughter. Then one day it all changed."

An ominous rumble of thunder echoed in the background as she continued. "Our father recorded things like holidays and birthday parties. After Michael's tenth birthday, the recordings all stopped. In fact, it seemed like all time stopped for our family. My father said something to Michael that day, but with all the noise at his birthday party I couldn't make out what it was. Later, he and Uncle Dick did something I never saw them do before. They started drinking hard liquor, right out of the bottle. After Michael's party, I helped my mother clean up the dining room and wash the dishes.

"Later a thunderstorm had started and my mother went into her sewing room to work on some mending. I didn't see Michael anywhere and started to panic because I couldn't find him. I climbed the back stairway, walking down the hall, looking into each of the rooms along the way. Then I heard his painful screams…'Stop hurting me! Stop hurting me! Stop!' I couldn't hear him too well because the sound of the thunder was muffling his screams." Then Grace buried her face in her hands and began to cry.

"Did they have to abuse my brother? He didn't do anything to them!" Grace was still crying when Cindy moved her chair next to her, putting one of her arms around her shoulder.

Jenny closed her notebook. She waited until Grace's crying subsided, then spoke softly. "Do you want to stop?"

Grace took a deep breath, shaking her head no. "After his screams stopped, there was a strange silence. My dad and uncle staggered out of my parents' bedroom, trying to straighten their pants and shirts. They stumbled down the stairs, out the front door onto the porch, passing out in two separate chairs. I know, because I followed them down the stairs and watched them go out there. Then I turned and ran back up the stairs to the second floor hallway. I stopped in front of my parents' bedroom door. Hearing nothing, I opened the door and went in.

"I held my hands over my mouth to keep from screaming out loud. Michael was facedown on my parents' bed. His hands were tied to the bedposts with clothesline. He had nothing on except a white T-shirt. I knew they had hurt him because his blood had soaked into it. He slowly turned his head to me, whispering in pain, 'Grace…please help me… please.'

"I untied him, helped him off the bed, taking him down the hall to the bathroom. I told him I was going to get our mother, but he kept begging me not to leave him alone. I found my mother, telling her what had happened. She ran upstairs to the bathroom where she started crying and hugging Michael. Then she carefully cleaned his wounds, putting some kind of salve on them from a first aid kit she had.

"After that day our lives changed. Michael would hardly speak to or go near my father or uncle. Whenever they would drink together, He and I would run and hide at the old mill that we played in. I never really blamed my mother because she couldn't have heard what was going on from her sewing room. I did often wonder why she didn't take him to the hospital or report it to the police. Maybe she was in denial or scared of my father and uncle; I don't know. I do know Michael blamed her, because he thought she should have protected him in some way or made sure it would never happen again.

"Two years later, our dad and uncle were killed in a hunting accident. At their funeral, Michael was sitting between me and our mother, looking down at the floor. He had a distant, angry look on his face, never looking at our father and uncle in their caskets. Aunt Ruth was sitting on the other side of me. She leaned over behind me whispering to him, asking if he would like to go up and look at his father and uncle for the last time. He jumped up, screaming at her out of the rage he held inside. 'I don't ever want to see them again!' He turned and faced our mother, still shouting. 'I'm glad they're both dead!' Then he ran out of the funeral home with me right behind him.

"I finally caught up with him two blocks away. He was in an alley, sitting on an old wooden crate with his arms wrapped around himself, crying. I sat down next to him on the crate and put my arms around him. I didn't say anything, I just held him. I know that what he did shocked and hurt our mother and Aunt Ruth. I also know my mother tried to make it up to him, but she died before he had the chance to forgive her." Her voice trailed off into a whisper. "I don't have anything more to say."

The only sound heard in the room was Cindy's quiet sobbing, along with the sound of rumbling thunder. Jenny spoke softly to Grace. "Okay, that's enough for today. You've dug up enough hurt. I have just one question. Do you have any other relatives that I might be able to talk to?"

Grace paused, staring at the rain hitting the office window. Then she looked at Jenny. "Michael's grandmother Rachael and her sister Catherine are still alive. They live on the family farm, twenty miles south of here in Manchester."

Jenny nodded. "With your permission, I'd like to talk to them. Maybe they can give me some information to form a basis where the emotional and mental patterns of abuse started in your family."

Grace rubbed her eyes. "Of course, if there's anything else I can do, just let me know."

Jenny responded. "Grace, eventually you'll want to forgive your dad and uncle for what they did to your brother."

Grace looked at her. "Yes, maybe eventually. Right now, forgiving them is the last thing on my mind, but if that's what it takes to get out of the emotional prison I'm in, then yes, I will. But I can't do that just yet" she continued, shaking her head. "I just can't."

Jenny directed her attention to Cindy, who had been quietly crying. "As a counselor I should not be involved in this case in any way, but Michael is my friend and I am not going to let our friendship get in the way of my objective reasoning. It's going to be hard, but I can do it. Years ago when Michael and I were going to college, he helped me through the emotional mess I was in when I lost my parents in a car accident. I promised I would help him if he ever needed me. Now he does and I'm keeping that promise."

She looked out of the office window. "It looks like the storm is starting to clear up. Let's go get something to eat and get our minds off this for a little while." Later after a delicious meal, they set up a time where they could all get together again.

Grace drove out of the parking lot, waving at Cindy and Jenny. Cindy waved back, then turned facing Jenny. "Jenny, what am I going to tell Michael when I get home?"

Jenny thought for a minute. "Tell him I want to see him for a separate session, but nothing else. He may ask a lot of questions, but you will have to hold your ground and not answer him. In the meantime, you and I should drive down to Manchester. Can you meet me here around ten thirty this coming Monday morning?"

Cindy pulled her day planner out of her purse and looked through it. "I don't see any reason I couldn't, but I will let you know at church tomorrow if I can't." Cindy turned to leave, then turned back to Jenny and hugged her. "Thank you, Jenny, for being there for Michael, Grace, and me. You're a good friend."

Jenny hugged her back. "That's what good friends are for. They help each other. Now I have to get home and feed my hungry family."

When Cindy arrived home, she found Michael sitting in the kitchen nook reading one of his favorite plane magazines. "The session went well. Oh! I see you got the stew out and heated it up. You want to share some with me?"

Michael grinned. "Sure, why not? I can't think of anyone else I'd rather share it with." After saying a short prayer, they began to eat.

After a while, Michael looked inquisitively at

Cindy. She sighed. "I can see the questions written all over your face, but Jenny told me not to answer any of them, and I agree with her. She's going to call you soon, and set up a time for the two of you to get together, and she'll answer everything you want to ask. How does that sound?"

Michael nodded. "It sounds okay with me. Let's clean up here and make some popcorn. Abby has been after us to watch a movie with her and Sarah."

The next day was Sunday. After church was over, Michael, Cindy, Jenny, and Dan, her husband, along with their daughters, stopped for lunch at the bistro in town. The men talked about getting together with the other pilots in their group to work on their planes. Cindy and Jenny sat talking quietly about what they were going to do on Monday. The girls amused themselves with coloring the place mats.

Later that evening, Cindy took a shower and got into bed. As usual she was reading a book. As Michael walked into the room, rubbing his head with a towel, she smiled at him. "Bet you can't guess who just called."

Michael stopped rubbing his head. "No, I can't." Cindy put her book down. "It was our daughter Chris." Michael's eyes widened. "How is she? Is she doing okay in college? How…"

Cindy smiled. "She's doing fine, but her dorm was gutted by fire. All she could save was her laptop computer, her purse, and some of her clothes. The rest of her things were lost in the fire. She is staying with one of her girlfriends off campus. From what she told me, the college is going to send her home until other housing arrangements can be made.

"She's coming home tomorrow morning on the ferry and I'll pick her up around nine. Jenny and I are going to Manchester to visit some people and Chris will go with us. We'll be back tomorrow evening, so you'll have to heat up the leftover stew for you and the girls. Are you okay with that?"

Michael smiled. "Sure, I guess I have to wait to give my big kid a hug." He gave her a suspicious stare. "Why are you going to Manchester? Are you going to see Grandma Rachael and her sister?"

Cindy sighed. "Yes. Jenny has a few questions she wants to ask them, and maybe I can talk Grandma Rachael out of some of that famous baked chicken she makes, along with one of her great blackberry pies you like."

Michael laughed. "Okay you got my arm twisted right down to my stomach. Anyway, let's get some sleep; it looks like we both have a full day ahead of us tomorrow."

Two Sisters

"A wise judge may let mercy temper justice but may not let mercy undo it."

Lewis B. Smedes - The Art of Forgiving:
When You Need To Forgive And Don't Know How

The next morning the sun rose slowly over the back of the hangar, chasing the dew off the grass around the house. Cindy had just finished up the breakfast dishes, and Michael had taken off in his plane. Janice had just picked up Sarah for day care and Abby had boarded her school bus. Cindy looked at the old regulator clock, doing a double take. It was already eight fifteen! She grabbed her purse off the kitchen table along with her coat. She walked over to the back door, glancing at the answering machine on the counter, making sure it was on.

Cindy walked out the back door of the kitchen and locked the door. She walked over to the station wagon, got in and started it. She drove out of the driveway onto County Road Seventeen. She was looking forward to picking up her oldest daughter.

Cindy drove the station wagon into a parking space near the Water Street ferry docks. It was fifteen minutes to nine and the ferry was docking. Cindy got out of the station wagon, walking over to where the ferry unloaded its passengers. About ten minutes later, Chris came off wearing a backpack, and dragging a suitcase on wheels that one of her friends let her use. When she saw her mom, she let go of it and ran into her mom's open arms. Cindy smiled. "It's sure good to see you, hon." She started to look her over. "No bruises, no cuts, no burns, anything broken?" Chris laughed. "Not even a fingernail."

Cindy thought about her last remark. "I'm just glad you got out alive, let alone break any of your fingernails." Chris sighed, letting go of her mother. "Mom, how is Dad? You didn't say too much on the phone, but I could tell it was serious by the tone of your voice."

"He's not that good, Chris." Cindy reached down, grabbed the handle of her daughter's suitcase, and started pulling it. She walked only a short distance when she stopped and looked at Chris. "I forgot to tell you that Jenny Peterson and I are going to visit your father's grandma and her sister today. We both thought it would be good if you came along with us. Jenny is going to ask them some questions about your dad's side of the family."

They walked a little farther when Chris stopped and looked at Cindy. "I really want to see Dad. Can't this wait another day?"

"No, sweetheart, I'm afraid it can't. You'll see your dad later on tonight. Is that okay?"

Chris sighed. "I guess it'll have to be. Just one thing though. Can we stop somewhere and get something to eat? I'm starving." Cindy laughed. "I just called Grandma Rachael while I was waiting for you to let her know that you might be coming. She said she'll make dinner for us, and knowing her, she will not let you leave hungry."

After they loaded the suitcase and backpack into the station wagon, they got in and drove into downtown Crandon. Soon Cindy turned the station wagon into the parking lot behind Jenny's office, parking it next to Jenny's car. Jenny had just come out of her office. She walked over to the side of the car where Chris sat, opened the door, and pulled her out, giving her a big hug.

"Hey, it's been ages since I saw you." She scrutinized Chris. "You didn't get hurt in any way in that fire, did you?" Chris answered, "No, I didn't, thank God." Jenny stared at her again. "Are you coming with us?" Chris sighed. "Yes, but I have some questions about my dad I need answered."

Jenny smiled and motioned to her car. "Good! On the way there you can ask as many as you like." They reached the outskirts of town when Jenny looked over at her. "So how have you been, Chris? What's new besides the usual college grind?"

Chris looked at her. "Well, I've been keeping a good grade point average. My classes are great, my professors are helpful, and I've got some great friends. Other than the fire which destroyed practically everything I owned, everything is cool."

Jenny kept her eyes on the road. "Did your mom fill you in on why we are going to visit your

Grandma Rachael and her sister?"

Chris looked at her, mentioning that she hadn't said too much. Jenny looked at her, glancing back and forth between her and the road. "I'm going to ask your grandma and her sister some questions about your dad, his father, and uncle." Jenny looked at Cindy sitting in the back seat through the rearview mirror. "Chris, both your mom and I feel that you should know what is going on with your dad. What I'm going to tell you is just between us three, Grace, your aunt, and no one else; is that understood?" Chris sighed. "What did happen to my dad?"

"Grace said that your dad was sexually abused when he was a small child by his dad and uncle." Chris turned away, looking out the window next to her, then back at Jenny with tears filling her eyes. "What did you just say?"

"Chris, from what your mom told me, your dad started acting strangely the night of a bad thunderstorm we had last week. I think the storm and a tape recording that he listened to earlier might have triggered some latent memories of his abuse buried deep in his mind. Everything that happens to your dad from now on is going to be like an emotional snowball rolling down hill.

"He'll need a good support team. Personally, I think he has one of the best." Chris turned and looked out the window again, wiping the tears out of her eyes with her hands. "This is going to cause my dad a lot of pain, isn't it?"

Jenny glanced at her, then back at the road. "Yes, but it can't be helped. Sooner or later the truth will force its way to the surface in everyone's life. Along with it comes change and refinement. Together they will make you resilient, enabling you to handle just about anything that the world sets on your plate and forces you to eat." Soon they reached the outskirts of Manchester, turning off the main highway onto a very bumpy gravel road. Chris exclaimed, "Whoa! What do they call this road? Crater Boulevard?" All the women were laughing as they came to a very old but well-kept farm on their left.

    Cindy pointed out the window. "This is it! Turn by the mailbox next to the big oak tree." Jenny turned left into a long, winding driveway that ended up at a quaint, three-story Victorian farmhouse surrounded by old lilac bushes and majestic oak and maple trees. In back of the house stood a big red barn with a fenced in barnyard, two outbuildings, and a chicken coop.

    Jenny stopped her car in front of the farmhouse. All three women sat in silence admiring the morning glories that were growing around the old porch posts. Soon two elderly women came out the front door and down the porch steps to Jenny's car. Jenny opened her car window. Cindy leaned over the front seat and said hello to each of them. Grandma Rachael looked down into the car. "Catherine and I are so happy that all of you came!"

    She looked at Chris sitting on the other side of the car and smiled. "The last time I saw you, young lady, you were a teenager." She looked at Jenny. "And you must be Jenny, Michael's friend from college."

Once inside Rachael, took their coats, hanging them up in a closet next to the door that opened onto the porch. She turned to Cindy. "I hope all of you are planning to stay for dinner." Cindy looked at her. "Yes, we wouldn't pass up your cooking for anything." Rachael smiled. "That's good, because my sister and I have been working most of the morning on it." Rachael put one of her forefingers to her lips. "Cindy, don't let me forget to give you a fresh blackberry pie along with some baked chicken to take home to Michael. If I remember right, they're two of his favorites."

Then Rachael clapped her hands together. "Now, let's go into the parlor where we can talk."

All the women walked into the parlor just off the dining room. It was a pleasant, sunlit room filled with family memories and overstuffed furniture. As the women sat down, Catherine turned to Cindy. "So what's new with your family, Cindy?" Cindy looked over at Jenny, who gave her a "be careful of what you say" stare. Cindy looked back at Catherine. "Well, everyone back home is fine. Michael is still flying the mail back and forth to the mainland along with anybody or anything else he can get into his plane. Abby is doing great in school, and Sarah is growing up faster than I want her to. Riley, our dog, is doing okay and so is Teaser, our cat. Our small business, the 'Practical Shop', is doing well, and Chris will tell you what is going on with her."

Both of the sisters looked over at Chris, who smiled. "I'm doing great in college. I have lots of great girlfriends but no boyfriends." Then she widened her eyes. "But there are a lot of cute guys on campus!" All of the women laughed.

Cindy nudged Chris on. "Tell them why you came home." Chris sighed. "The dorm I was in caught fire and everything inside it burned. Everyone made it out okay, but all of us lost most of what we had. So the college sent all of us home because student housing was full. I have to call the administration office and find out how they are going to handle our classes. They said they were going to find housing for us as soon as possible, but I guess I'll have to wait and see."

Jenny shifted in her chair, causing the sisters to turn their attention to her. "I met Michael at the same college that Chris is going to right now. We immediately became best friends. At the time, I had lost my parents in a bad car accident. I was trying to cope with a full class load and grieving over the loss of my parents at the same time. Michael was an angel. He was there for me when I needed someone to talk to or a shoulder to cry on. I couldn't ask for a better friend."

Jenny looked over at Cindy. "Then this attractive and somewhat aggressive blonde stood up at a football game we were at and introduced herself to Michael with a kiss. After college, she became his wife and a good friend to me. What brings me here today is Michael. Cindy mentioned before that he's fine. Well, he isn't."

The sisters looked at each other and back at Jenny. "I'm a sexual abuse counselor. It's my job to help people cope with anything related to this type of trauma. Cindy came to my office last week along with Michael's sister Grace. They both shared some very emotional things with me regarding Michael, especially Grace. She told us that Michael was sexually abused by his father and uncle in the home he lives in now as a small boy."

All at once everyone in the room became strangely silent. Except for the ticking of a clock on the parlor wall, you could hear a pin drop. The sisters looked at each other with tears starting to form in their eyes. Finally Rachael cleared her throat. "I can't speak for my sister, but I had a feeling this was going to rear its ugly head sooner or later." She wiped the tears from her eyes with a handkerchief she had pulled from her apron pocket. "Michael's father Roger and his brother Dick were abused when they were small boys, by their father, Frank, and Steve, his brother. It didn't happen here. It happened in our home in Springfield, just west of Manchester. It was during a bad thunderstorm, and Catherine and I were at a church meeting. We had no idea what had happened until we got home that night. We found Frank and Steve passed out in chairs on the front porch, with their pants half fastened.

"They had both been drinking all the time we were at church. We were furious at them for drinking themselves into a drunken stupor. We decided to let them sleep it off right there on the front porch. We became concerned for Roger and Dick. We couldn't find them anywhere in the house, so we went out to the garage."

Rachael looked tearfully at her sister. "I can't say any more." Catherine sighed, wiping her eyes with a handkerchief. "When my sister and I opened the garage door, we held our hands to our mouths to keep from screaming. Both her sons were tied by their hands with rope to a large hook, on a support board in the back of the garage. Their pants were pulled down and they both had blood on their backsides. They were crying and saying things that didn't make any sense at all.

"We ran up to them, untied them, and carried them into the house to the bathroom. We gently cleaned them and took them to the hospital. After the doctor examined and treated them, he took us into a separate room. He told us that they had been abused and he was going to report it to the police. The police came, spoke to the doctor and then to us. They told us that our husbands should be arrested. We were so angry we agreed with them.

"Later that morning the police picked up Frank and Steve and took them to jail. It was the hardest thing to send our husbands there but we did. To make a long story short, we ended up divorcing them. They both got into some other trouble after that and got sentenced to prison. After that, we never saw them again. Part of me died when my husband was incarcerated, and I am sure part of my sister did too. We eventually sold our house in Springfield, moved out here with the boys, and finished raising them here. Roger became a pilot and served in Korea. Steve also served in Korea as a tank commander. After the war, they came back home and married their high school sweethearts. Roger bought the house that Michael and Cindy own now. It needed a lot of work, but he and his wife did a good job in fixing it up. Steve and his wife moved just down the road from them and renovated a cute little Cape Cod house. The rest of this story you know." Catherine's voice trailed off into a whisper that ended in silence.

Jenny sighed. "I think that's enough for today. I don't want you two to dredge up any more hurt than you already have. However, if you do remember anything else, I'll give you my office and cell phone number. I'd appreciate it if you could call me with anything that you haven't already told me."

Then Jenny sniffed the air. "Is that roast chicken I smell?" Rachael's eyes widened. "It sure is, sister, come help me with it." All the women got up, walking into the dining room where Rachael pointed to a buffet. "Cindy, you'll find cloth napkins and silverware in that buffet and plates, cups, and saucers in that china cabinet. By the time you get the table ready, we should have the food ready." Soon the table was set and the food brought in from the kitchen. As the women sat down, Rachael looked at Cindy, asking her to pray. Cindy began: "Father, we thank you for loving us. Help us to forgive those who have hurt us in the past, Amen."

Catherine spoke up. "Well, help yourselves. There's plenty to go around." The meal was delicious and the conversation was lively. After dessert everyone pitched in with washing and drying the dishes. Jenny was putting away the last of the silverware when she looked down at her wristwatch and back at Cindy. "I think we should be going home."

Jenny got their coats out of the closet and gave

Cindy and Chris theirs. As they were going out the door, Rachael handed Chris the pie and baked chicken for Michael. Everyone was saying their goodbyes when Cindy walked up to Grandma Rachael and hugged her. As she turned to leave, Rachael grabbed her coat sleeve. "Cindy, I know in my heart that God is in the past, the present, and the future. He'll see that everything will turn out right, don't you think?"

Cindy hugged her again. "Yes, I truly believe he will."

On the way home nothing was said until they got into the outskirts of Crandon. Cindy spoke first. "Jenny, when are you going to talk to Michael?" Jenny glanced at her, then back at the road. "Soon, I hope, but I have to go over all my notes before I do. If Michael asks you any questions, just say we visited and had a wonderful dinner."

Soon Jenny drove her car into a parking space behind her office. She turned, looking at Cindy. "What would you say if I had the sessions at your house, Cindy?" Cindy looked at Chris, who shrugged her shoulders, then back at Jenny. "I don't mind, but don't you think it might open up Michael's wounds too soon?" Jenny focused on Cindy.

"Cindy, when someone you love and trust violates you physically, it leaves a spiritual, mental, and emotional imprint. No matter how many years abuse victims bury these horrendous memories in their mind, they will surface sooner or later, triggered by something as simple as a thunderstorm." Jenny continued. "To answer your question, yes, it will open up his wounds. But they need to be opened. He has to face the cause of his pain sooner or later. I am debating whether or not to use his parents' old bedroom for the sessions. That's where he was abused. What do you two think?"

Cindy looked at her. "I don't think you could get him to physically go into that room for anything, let alone a session."

Jenny sighed. "Okay, let's make a few changes to the room. Lesson the effect of the memories he has of it."

Cindy and Chris only heard what they wanted to hear. "Yes, let's do it. I've wanted to get my hands on that room for years. Let's replace everything from wallpaper to rugs, curtains, and that godforsaken bed! That thing I will personally smash into pieces and burn."

Chris moved forward to the edge of the back seat. "We can paint the walls a soft yellow. We can hang art reproductions on the walls, and set potted plants or fresh flowers around the room!"

Jenny realized that they had missed her point entirely. Michael needed the exposure to this painful part of his past. She tapped her fingers on her car's steering wheel. She turned to Cindy and Chris. "Girls, please listen to me!" Both women stopped talking and looked at her. Jenny continued. "Okay, I can't drug Michael and drag him physically into that room. Since he won't go in there on his own, I'll have to find another source of pain to expose him to." She paused, staring at them. "And I can't stop you two from redoing that room; that's your choice. What I am wondering is who this is for, you two or him?"

Later when Cindy drove the station wagon into the carport at home, she looked at Chris. "Are you up to all this? Your dad is probably going to do some strange things. Our love for him is going to have to be just as strong as his hurt. One thing we might have to do is find a place for Sarah and Abby to stay temporarily if he starts to get physical, because they may not understand what he's going through."

Chris agreed, giving Cindy a questioning stare. "What if Dad thinks that he was to blame in some way for all that happened to him?" Cindy reached over and hugged her daughter. "Well, let's talk to God about it… Father, please help Michael understand that what happened to him that night wasn't his fault. Help Grace not to blame herself for not helping him more than she did. Help them both see that they need to forgive their father and uncle." Then she smiled. "Let's go in. Your dad is anxious to see you."

Michael was sitting at the table going over his itinerary for the next day when Cindy and Chris walked into the house. The minute they came in, he jumped up and ran over to his daughter.

"You don't know how good it is to see you!" he said, hugging her. Chris smiled up at him. "You don't know how wonderful it is to be held by the best dad in the whole world." Michael looked at her for a moment, then sighed. "I think you're right, I don't." Chris made a face, realizing what she said was partially true.

Cindy joined the conversation. "Well, how did

my stew taste?" Michael let go of Chris, walked over, and wrapped his arms around her.

"Your stew was terrific as usual. We ate all of it and licked the dishes clean." Cindy gave him a suspicious stare. "I hope you washed them afterwards." Michael's eyes twinkled. "Oh, we thought they were clean enough so we put them away like that."

"You did not, you big brat!"

Michael grinned. "Of course we didn't. We let Riley lick them clean!" Cindy made a face, swatting him with one of her hands, then looked at Chris. "Why don't you go upstairs and wake up your sisters and bring them down? I'll make some popcorn and we'll all catch up on things."

Chris left the kitchen, going up the back stairs. Soon Michael and Cindy heard a lot of laughing and squealing upstairs. Shortly after that Chris, Abby, and Sarah came down the back stairway. Michael let go of Cindy, touching her cheek with one of his hands. "I missed you today."

Cindy smiled, then widened her eyes. "Oh, I almost forgot; Grandma Rachael made you a blackberry pie and some baked chicken. It's in the station wagon." Michael sniffed the air. "Yum, I can smell it from here." He turned, walking out the back door grabbing his car keys on his way out. Cindy had just turned on a stove burner to heat water in the kettle when the phone rang. Cindy walked over and answered the phone call from Jenny, who was checking in to see how things were going.

Later, around two in the morning, Cindy

glanced over at the clock on the wall. "I don't know about the rest of you, but I'm tired." Michael yawned and stretched. "I've got to get some sleep. I have a heavy workload today and I may not make it back here until later in the evening."

Chris took her dad's cue, looking at her sisters. "Okay, you two, I'll race you up to bed!" Off they ran up the stairs, laughing and squealing.

The Barnstormers

"We forgive freely or we do not really forgive at all."
Lewis B. Smedes - The Art of Forgiving:
When You Need To Forgive And Don't Know How

Once a year, Michael and six other pilots got together and worked on their planes, swapping plane parts, stories, and friendship. It was

Michael's turn to host this yearly event, and he was looking forward to seeing his fellow aviators. Michael's small group got their name from the dangerous stunt of barnstorming that some pilots would attempt back in the 1920s. These early pilots would fly their airplanes through one open end of a huge barn and out the other. However, this group of flyers was more interested in keeping their planes flying and less interested in attacking barns with them.

On the Friday following Chris's homecoming, the men started to arrive in their planes. One by one they landed, parking close together near Michael's hangar. The men also brought their wives and children with them, making it more like a family reunion than a plane meet. After all the aircraft landed and everyone had said their hellos, they all sat down at long folding tables and feasted.

Cindy, Chris, and Grace (who Michael had invited to stay with them for a while) made several dishes of food. They had just set them out when one of the pilots walked up and smiled at Grace.

Grace smiled back. "Hi, you must be Dave Nelson." Dave widened his eyes. "Yes, I am. How did you know my name?"

"You're wearing a name tag."

Dave laughed. "Right, and what's yours?"

"I'm Grace Jacobson, Michael's sister." Dave smiled, looking deep into her eyes. "Imagine that, Michael keeping someone as pretty as you a secret."

Grace blushed. "Here, have some potato salad."

As Dave walked off with his plate of food, Cindy went up next to Grace, whispering in her ear. "Dave is single, Grace. He is the youth group leader at church and has his own appliance repair shop in town." Grace followed Dave with her eyes, then turned, looking at Cindy. "You wouldn't happen to have his phone number, would you?"

Cindy laughed. "It's in the church directory in the house."

Later after everyone finished eating, the men went to work repairing each other's planes. The women and children picked up the dishes, took them into the kitchen, and started to wash them up. Once the dishes were done and put away, the children went outside to play with strict instructions not to go anywhere near the planes that their fathers were working on. Soon the children were playing under the watchful eyes of Grace and Chris. The other women, including Cindy and Jenny, climbed the back stairway, walking down the hallway to Michael's parents' old bedroom.

The first part of the room's planned renovation was to get rid of the old four-poster bed. The women took it down the stairs in pieces and out the back door, throwing it along with the old mattress on the trash heap to be burned. The rest of the room's furniture was taken up to the attic to be stored and later sold to an antique dealer. Then the women started cleaning and removing all the old wallpaper and curtains. After the wallpaper was removed with the steamer they rented, it was thrown along with old clothing onto a worn-out Oriental rug. They rolled up the rug, taking it out to the same trash heap as the old bed. Any valuables or personal items of Michael's parents were put into cardboard boxes, labeled, and stored in the attic.

While all this was happening, Michael looked up only once from one of the planes he was working on. He saw the women carrying out the different items from the house, assuming they were doing some spring housecleaning. Shrugging his shoulders, he stared at them, trying to ignore the sick feeling in his stomach. Later in the day, Cindy looked at Jenny, making a time-out sign with her hands. Jenny put two fingers in her mouth and whistled above the noise of all the talking women. The women stopped their work and looked at her.

Jenny announced, "It's starting to get dark out, ladies, so I suggest we quit for today and start early tomorrow right after breakfast; is that okay? All the women agreed as Cindy went over the sleeping arrangements for everyone.

When she finished, she glanced out a nearby window towards the hangar. "I'm not sure, but it looks like the guys are starting to migrate toward the house in search of food. Let's leave all the cleaning stuff in the room and lock it up." Cindy smiled and looked around the room. "Thanks to all of you, we've got a lot done today."

The women left the room, talking and leaning their mops and brooms up against one wall. Jenny was the last to leave. She stopped, heaving a sigh of relief. "Good riddance, you Pandora's Box of a room; I sure won't miss you."

She closed the door behind her, turning off the light as she did. She locked the door, handing the key to Cindy. Later, after everyone else had taken their showers and gone to bed, Cindy and Michael were sitting alone in the kitchen talking over what went on during the day. Michael suddenly sighed and looked at Cindy.

"What's happening to me? I feel like I'm going to explode and a lot of crud is going to come flying out of me."

Cindy looked at him with her eyes tearing up. "I know, sweetheart. I saw it coming weeks ago."

She reached over, drew him into her arms and kissed him. Michael looked back at her, trying hard but failing to hold in his emotions. "I saw you girls carrying out all that stuff from the house. It made me sick just to look at it."

He paused, then sighed. "That wasn't the worst

part. I was working on my plane and just closed the cover to one of the engines. I turned around and there was my dad and uncle staring right at me with liquor bottles in their hands. I know they're both dead, but they seemed so real I could almost smell the alcohol on their breath!"

Michael sighed again, wiping off the sweat forming on his forehead. "I started to shake, dropping the wrench I had in my hand. Pastor Jim saw the look on my face. He came over and put his arm around me, asking me if I was okay. He told me, 'I think you just pulled something frightening out of that mind of yours.'

"I was still shaking when I looked at him. He stood there looking at me with a strange look on his face, like he saw right through me to the hurt inside." Cindy stood up, kissing Michael on one side of his face. "Let's go to bed, sweetheart. You and the other guys have got a long day ahead of you tomorrow. Why don't you try to forget what you saw today and get some sleep?" Michael nodded, following her up the back stairway.

The Howling

"We attach our feelings to the moment when we were hurt, endowing it with immortality. And we let it assault us every time it comes to mind. It travels with us, sleeps with us, hovers over us while we make love, and broods over us while we die. Our hate does not even have the decency to die when those we hate die--for it is a parasite sucking OUR blood, not theirs. There is only one remedy for it. [forgiveness]

Lewis B. Smedes - The Art of Forgiving:
When You Need To Forgive And Don't Know How

Around midnight when everyone was in bed, sound asleep, the wind picked up around the old mill. It howled as it blew through the trees around it, causing them to sway and twist in some sort of ancient dance. It blew unopposed throughout the old building in a screaming chorus of a thousand voices.

It swirled around and around, picking up the debris and dust on the mill's floor fashioning it into grotesque human-like forms. These frightful caricatures danced furiously around the old millstones, then flew shrieking out of the old building, slamming the wooden door against its frame. The wind scattered in all directions across the inland lake, whipping the water into an almost uncontrollable frenzy, then bent trees in all directions as it flew through the forest, across the meadow toward the house. It pushed its way through the trees in the yard, grabbing them with its windy hands, snapping off some of their branches.

Lightning and thunder followed, along with the rain that started with a sprinkle here and there, then a downpour. Jenny sat straight up, wide awake in bed, at the first crash of thunder. She turned on the night-light next to the bed and got up, trying not to wake anyone. Putting on her bathrobe, she walked to the bedroom door, opened it, and turned on the hall lights.

She noticed Cindy coming out of the bathroom door that opened into the hallway. "Cindy, is Michael still in bed?"

Cindy looked at her, rubbing her eyes with her hands. "No! I don't know where he is!"

Jenny held Cindy by her shoulders. "When did he get out of bed?" Cindy looked down at the floor for a moment, then back up at Jenny. "Wait a minute! He got up and got dressed when the wind started blowing about an hour ago!"

Jenny let go of Cindy. "Go get dressed and wake up Chris and Grace!"

Cindy ran over to the bedroom where Chris and Grace were sleeping and woke them up. All the women scrambled to get their clothes on before they rushed down the back stairs into the kitchen, turning on the lights. It was still storming outside when the women left the house and got into the station wagon. Cindy looked at Jenny, shaking her head. "No, you don't think he could've gone there…"

Jenny looked at her. "I think you know he could. Let's get to the mill as soon as we can!"

Cindy put the station wagon in gear, driving it out of the carport, across the runway, and onto the old logging road that led to the old mill. No one said a word until a big tree limb suddenly broke and crashed down in front of them. All the women screamed as Cindy slammed both feet down on the brake pedal!

Jenny shouted. "Come on! We've got to move that limb!" The women got out and struggled to move the limb to the side of the road. Tired, wet, and wasting precious time, they got back in the station wagon. The wind continued to whip tree limbs against the windshield of the station wagon, sometimes blocking Cindy's view of the road. Eventually the shape of the old mill appeared in the vehicle's headlights, silhouetted now and then by intermittent flashes of lightning. The rain was still falling when Cindy turned the motor off. They sat in silence for a short while listening to the wind, the rain, and the thunder, looking at the old structure standing menacingly in front of them.

Jenny sighed. "Okay, let's find out if he is in there." The four women got out of the station wagon, turning on the flashlights they were carrying. Between flashes of lightning and rumbles of thunder, they heard an eerie cry followed by low guttural moaning. It sounded more like a wounded animal than anything human. Suddenly a piercing scream caused the women to run as fast as they could to the entrance of the old mill. They threw open its door and ran inside.

They ran through the mill and up the back stairs to the small room where the scream came from. Stopping in front of the door, they wiped the water off their faces. Jenny carefully but swiftly opened it.

There, lying on the dirty floor, was Michael. He had covered himself in an old moth-eaten blanket and lay there moaning and crying. An old kerosene lantern that he had lit revealed the cuts and bruises he had gotten from falling on sharp objects in the logging road. Cindy held her hands to her mouth, holding in her emotions. Chris looked at Cindy and Jenny. She started over to him, but was held back by Jenny who looked at her, shaking her head no.

Jenny pointed to her flashlight, turning it off as a signal for the other women. She had to think quickly. Because of his hurts, Michael's mind had slipped somewhere into his past. Jenny whispered something into Grace's ear.

Grace nodded, turned, and walked slowly towards Michael, stopping within a few feet of him. "Michael, it's your sister, Grace. Can I help you?"

Michael stopped moaning, looked at her, and cried out. "I can't take this anymore! Please help me kill myself!" Michael slowly pulled an old, loaded pistol out from under the blanket he was covered in.

Grace swore to herself when she recognized the weapon. The memory of Michael hiding it in the mill when he was a small boy hit her like a slap across her face.

Grace thought quickly. She looked deep into his eyes, speaking as softly and as calmly as she could. "If I help you, can I hold the gun?"

Grace tried hard to control her shaking hands as she got down in front of Michael. He slowly handed her the weapon. Grace took the pistol from him and slowly pointed it to his head. Then in one swift movement of her hand, she threw it out a nearby open window.

Michael grabbed her shoulders, shouting, "Why did you do that!? I want to die!" Then he passed out.

Grace burst into tears and held him tight in her arms. "I love you too much to help you die!"

The other women rushed over and got down on the floor, wrapping their arms around Grace and Michael. Outside the mill, the storm began to subside along with the crying inside it. The rain became a slow drizzle; the wind, a softly blowing breeze.

Cindy was the first to move, followed by Chris, who got up and rubbed her eyes. Jenny slowly got up, smiling at Grace holding Michael in her lap. Jenny turned on her flashlight, blowing out the lantern on the table.

"Okay, let's get him out of here." Together the four women carefully picked up Michael's unconscious body and carried him out of the mill. They opened the back door to the station wagon, laying him on some blankets that were there. Cindy and Grace got in back with him, starting to clean his wounds with some antiseptic wipes they had. Chris got in front with Jenny, who drove them back down the old logging road to the house.

Jenny drove the vehicle into the carport, stopped, and turned off its motor. She turned on its interior lights, looking at Chris, then at the women in the back. She put her thumb and forefinger together. "You know that we were this close to losing him. We need to calm down and think about what happened tonight. Right now let's get Michael into the upstairs bathroom where we can get him cleaned up and into bed.

"Cindy, can you make up some excuse and tell everyone that Michael is sick, getting them all out of the house in the morning? That way Michael can sleep. Grace, you were wonderful. I can see why Michael loves you so much. You're a good sister who loves her brother."

Jenny and Chris got out of the station wagon. They opened the rear door, helping Cindy and Grace get Michael out. After the women got him inside, they carried him through the kitchen and down the hallway to the main staircase. As quietly as possible, they carried him up the stairs down the south hallway into the bathroom, where they carefully laid him on the floor.

Chris exhaled and whispered to her mom. "Whew! I didn't know Dad weighed this much!"

Cindy's face turned into a weak smile. "I'm guilty; it must be my cooking."

Jenny smiled. "This, ladies, is where I bow out. He's all yours, Cindy. I'm going to dry off, then crawl in bed with my husband, hoping he didn't notice I was gone." Jenny left the bathroom along with Chris and Grace. Cindy sat down on the edge of the tub. She could've used their help with Michael. She was tired and had no idea how she was going to get him into the tub by herself. She knelt down on the floor next to him and started unbuttoning his shirt. Suddenly Michael's eyes blinked open and he pushed himself up into a sitting position against the wall.

He looked at Cindy, a weak smile forming on his face. "How did I end up here? The last thing I remember, I was in bed. Now I am sitting on the bathroom floor, fully dressed and totally soaked." He slowly got up and looked into the mirror above the sink. "Wow! Who or what tried to beat me to death?"

Cindy sighed and got up off the floor. She stood beside him with her eyes tearing up. "A part of your past did, that's what. If Grace hadn't done what she did, you might not be staring at yourself in the mirror right now." Michael turned and stared at her. He had no idea what she was talking about because he had buried everything inside his mind again. Cindy sighed. "Let's get you into the shower. After you're through, I'll take mine. After that, I'll patch you up and put you to bed."

Later that morning Cindy woke up to the sound of aircraft engines starting up. She yawned and got out of bed, being careful not to wake Michael, who was still sleeping. She put on her bathrobe and slippers and walked down the back stairway into the kitchen. Grace and Chris were cleaning up the breakfast dishes.

Cindy walked over to a kitchen window, watching the planes take off. When the last plane was in the air, she turned, looking at Chris. "Why did you let me sleep through the morning? I wanted to say goodbye to all of them."

Chris looked at her. "Mom, we decided to let you sleep in. Heaven knows you needed it. Besides, Grace handled it perfectly, didn't you, Grace?"

Grace looked up from her coffee mug. "Well, I just told them that Michael got sick during the night and that you had stayed up with him and needed the sleep. I guess that was okay with them. Right after breakfast they said their goodbyes, packed up their tools and families in their planes, and took off.

"Jenny told Abby and Sarah that they could spend the rest of the summer with April and Maggie. She said that she'd drive back over later today and discuss what we should do next with Michael. Sarah and Abby flew back home with Dan and Jenny, excited that they were going to spend time having fun with their friends."

Cindy focused her attention on Grace. "Grace, there's something I've wanted to ask you since we first talked to Jenny in her office. I was wondering if you would consider moving in with us. I know you have your own house up north, but you and Michael have been away from each other so long that..." Cindy paused. "What I'm trying to say is: Michael's wounded. Michael is going to need you more than ever now. You don't have to give me an answer right now; just think about it for a while."

Grace looked at Cindy, tapping her fingers on the table. "I know I haven't seen Michael, you, or your daughters for years. I guess I didn't want to go near this house. But when I saw my brother on that mill floor trying to take his life with that old pistol, I knew without a doubt that I needed him more than he might need me. Besides, living in the house I have now is probably an excuse to keep running away from the truth."

She smiled at Cindy. "Yes, I'll move in with you. That is, if you think you can put up with me."

Cindy went around the table, pulled Grace out of her chair, and hugged her. Outside the house, a sudden blast of wind caused the mattress from the old bed to slide off the trash heap; a visible sign that the dark shadows of the past would soon creep in again.

Skeletons In The Closet

"He that cannot forgive others, breaks the bridge over which he himself must pass if he would reach heaven; for everyone has need to be forgiven." Lance Morrow - (article, Time Magazine, January 9, 1984)

Later that afternoon Michael was still asleep. All three women were down in the kitchen talking about the renovation of the old bedroom upstairs. Soon they heard a car door closing, then someone knocking on the back door.

Cindy looked up. "Door's open, come on in."

Jenny opened the back door and walked in, carrying her overnight bag. She set it down as she looked at the other women. "Is Michael still sleeping?"

Chris yawned and stretched. "Yes, he is. Can I help you carry anything in from your SUV?"

Jenny looked at her. "I have two more suitcases out there but they can wait. We need to talk before your father wakes up." She looked over at the stove. "Got any fresh coffee over there?"

As Grace got up to get her coffee, Jenny sat

down at the table in the nook opposite Chris and Cindy. Looking at them, she pulled a thick manila folder from the briefcase she was carrying and laid it on the table in front of her.

"First of all, I want to thank all three of you for agreeing to let me stay here. Now when Michael wakes up, he probably won't remember what happened at the mill. He might ask about the cuts and bruises he has, but that's about it. In the past, Michael has had to protect himself emotionally and mentally against the trauma he suffered as a child. As a result, he's mentally short-circuited the memories of what happened to him.

"He's locked up all that hurt so deep in his mind that no one, except God or someone that has my experience and training, can unlock it."

Grace came over from the stove and set a cup of hot coffee in front of Jenny. "The trigger mechanisms are what they are. A smell, a photo, or an everyday happening could suddenly become the connection that could cause him to remember the very thing his mind is trying to suppress."

Jenny glanced at Grace sitting next her to in the nook. Then she gave Cindy and Chris a serious look. "I'm sorry, you two, but I'm going to start opening up Michael's wounds earlier then I had planned. His flashbacks are happening more frequently, and it's starting to concern me. Take the fiasco at the mill earlier this morning. For starters, we were totally unaware that he left the house. He ran down the logging road where he could have fallen and hurt himself worse than he did. Once he got to the mill, he dug up that old pistol that Grace forgot he had hidden there."

She paused. "As much as I hate to say it, we should probably keep him from flying. If he's up in the air by himself and something triggers a flashback, he could crash." She looked at Cindy, then, at Chris and Grace. "Does anyone have any ideas how to keep Michael grounded?"

Chris looked down, then at Jenny. "Wait a minute. I've been taking flying lessons and passed the licensing requirements for piloting a small, twin-engine aircraft."

Cindy turned, giving her a surprised look. "My, aren't you one for surprises!"

Chris smiled awkwardly. "I'm sorry that I didn't tell you, but they offered the lessons at college and I decided to take them. Why can't I take over for Dad this summer?"

Cindy glared at her daughter. "Yes, if Dave flies with you! You don't have enough experience flying your father's plane, and until you get your pilot's license, I don't want to see you near it!"

"Well, the plane I took flying lessons in was a twin-engine Cessna. I don't see too much difference between it and Dad's plane," countered Chris.

Jenny folded her hands behind her head and spoke. "I think she could. Once she gets her license and logs enough flight hours, I don't see any problem in her taking over for her dad."

Cindy thought of something else. "I have a better idea. She can start flying with her father. That way if something does happen, she can take over for him. Michael knows his plane better than anyone else and can show her everything she needs to know. How does that sound?"

Jenny reached for her coffee cup on the table. "I don't know. If Michael gets physical, Chris couldn't handle him and the plane at same time. It's too much of a risk."

Chris looked at Jenny and sighed. "You're right, Jenny, it is; but I love my father, making it a risk that I am willing to take."

Grace changed the subject with the news of a potential buyer. "Well, I think I have a buyer my house. Molly and Jack Stilwell's son and new wife are looking for a starter home. His son said they were pre-approved for a home loan but hadn't found anything in their price range. I think I'll call them right now and make them an offer."

As Grace walked over to the phone, Jenny looked at Chris and Cindy still sitting in the nook. "I've asked Sherrie Henderson, an old college chum of mine, to come down and handle some of my caseload for me while I am staying here with you. She said she would as long as she could stay at our house.

"I also called Janice Benson, who had her own gift shop at one time. She said she would run the 'Practical Shop' for us as long as we needed her to. That leaves the four of us to deal with whatever arises with Michael."

Grace finished talking on the phone. She came over and sat down at the table again. "Guess what! Mollie and Jack will show it to their son and daughter-in-law tomorrow. If they like it, Mollie will call me. If they decide to buy the house, I'll sell or give away most of my things other than my clothes and car. Now what did I miss while I was on the phone?"

Jenny explained what they had discussed.

Grace focused her attention on Jenny for a moment. "What do you mean by starting the wounding process?"

"I help him open up his buried memories and help him deal with the trauma that they have caused." She paused, then focused her attention on all three women. "What all of you have to realize is that, like other abuse victims, Michael suffered this emotional and physical trauma when he was a small child. A flashback or a body memory of this trauma can and will cause a very real conflict with his present-day mind, like trying to fit a square peg into a round hole. It could cause him to become very confused and totally disoriented. That's why abuse victims bury memories deep in their minds or numb their emotions so they don't have to re-experience the pain that comes with the memories."

Jenny spoke directly to Cindy and Chris. "Don't be surprised if Michael becomes controlling or loses his temper for no apparent reason. Rest assured, you are probably not the cause of it. Relational conflicts are a hallmark of this type of abuse." She paused. "To protect Michael, let's agree everything that goes on here from now on is kept a secret and if someone asks, we all say is that he is taking the summer off to relax. God knows that's not true but honestly, it's no one else's business."

All three women nodded their heads in agreement. Just then Michael came down the back stairway into the kitchen. He stood there yawning, stretching, and rubbing his eyes, still dressed in his pajamas. All the women turned looking at him standing there.

Cindy spoke to him first. "Hey, handsome, do you realize how long you've been sleeping?"

Michael made a face, scratching his head. "I am guessing for a week, right?"

Chris laughed. "Do you want something to eat? You have that 'feed me' look in your eyes." Michael sat down across the table from Jenny and smiled at her. Jenny sighed, realizing that he had buried everything that happened at the mill deep inside his mind again. She looked at Michael. "Don't you remember anything after you went to bed last night?"

Michael looked around the kitchen as he spoke. "No, not too much except…hey! Where are all the guys and their families? We had a lot of work left to do and…"

Cindy interrupted him. "Hon, we sent them all home earlier this morning." She looked at Jenny and back at Michael. "Please sit down. Jenny has some things that she'd like to share with you. The rest of us are going for a walk."

Michael watched as the three women got up and walked out the back door. Jenny smiled at him, patting the cushion on the bench seat she was sitting on with her hand. "Hey, you handsome hunk of a man, come on over here and sit next to me."

Michael smiled as he sat down on the bench seat. "I'm warning you, I have dragon breath."

To Jenny, Michael's trust in her was more important than his breath. "Michael, do you love and trust me as a friend and counselor?"

Michael smiled. "Now what brought that on? Of course I love and trust you that way. I know you are doing this for my own good. Besides, you and Dan have been good friends with Cindy and me for years. We love you both. We always will."

Jenny continued with a slight smile on her face. "I have to give Cindy credit. She sure is a fast mover. If she hadn't kissed you that day in that stadium I probably would've snagged you for myself."

Michael laughed, looking up at the ceiling, then back at her. "I'll take that as a compliment, but you were meant for Dan and you know it. Especially that day you and Dan met for the first time at that drive-in and you fell for him, literally, right between the cars."

Jenny laughed, grabbing his forearm with one of her hands. "Yes, now I remember! I was on my knees in the driver's seat trying to shake hands with him. I lost my balance and fell headfirst out of my convertible taking the tray, the food, and myself down in-between the two cars. I ended up wearing my food, but I also ended up marrying one of the cutest guys in the world."

Michael smiled. "And I could tell Dan was hooked on you by the way he was picking dirt-encrusted French fries out of your hair and eating them. No one in his right mind would do that. It was love at first bite. Now what was it that you wanted to talk to me about?"

Jenny grimaced slightly, then took her hand off his forearm. "Do you remember what you were going to say when I asked if you remembered anything about last night and you said 'not too much except'...except what?"

Michael looked away, then back at her. "Except I had a strange dream about Grace and I at the old mill and something about an old gun, but that's all I remember."

"Wait right here, Michael. I want Grace to hear what I'm going to say next." Michael watched her as she got up from the table, walking over to and out the back door. He shifted uneasily on the bench seat, like a little boy in a doctor's office waiting for his first booster shot.

Soon Grace and Jenny walked through the back door, followed by Cindy and Chris. Chris walked over and kissed her dad on his forehead, then walked out of the kitchen with her mom. Jenny walked over to the table, sitting down in a chair opposite Michael. Grace slid in next to Michael on the bench seat, wrapping both her hands around her brother's left forearm.

Jenny picked up the file folder and opened it looking at several of the typed sheets of paper then closed it and looked at Michael. "Michael, a lot of individuals may have dark secrets hidden in their past that they don't want exposed. That's because there are hurts associated with them that they don't want to face. To help expose yours I'll use a process that I call 'facing the skeletons in the closet.' Now when I mention skeleton, does that bother you in any way?"

Michael raised his eyebrows and shrugged his shoulders. "No, but it does remind me of the time that you and I stole 'Mr. Bones' out of the biology department at college. Do you remember that?"

As serious as Jenny was trying to be, she couldn't help but smile. "Yes I do, you big brat! We tried to find a place to stash him fast and ended up throwing him into a laundry hamper, covering him with dirty tablecloths from the cafeteria. He ended up going into town where a local dry cleaning crew went into hysterics when they found a skeleton mixed in with dirty laundry! What a mess!

"Of course, they had to call the police, who called the dean, and he called the biology professor, who called in all of us students! Nobody found out who stole him. I couldn't get over the look on the professor's face when two red-faced students, who are forever nameless, suddenly walked out of the biology department into separate bathrooms, where they went into severe laughing fits."

Jenny sighed. "We were a pair in those days. What you just said about Mr. Bones proves one of the points I was going to bring up. Funny stories and laughter are forms of healing, but in your case it can be an excuse for not dealing with the real problem." Michael and Grace stopped laughing as Jenny started asking some very pointed questions.

"Michael, in one word, what does that bedroom of your parents upstairs mean to you?"

Michael looked at Grace, then back at Jenny, and sighed. "Pain, it means pain to me." Tears were starting to form in Grace's eyes as she held Michael's forearm.

Jenny concentrated her stare at him as tears began to fill his eyes. "What kind of pain, Michael?"

"I don't remember what kind of pain." Jenny

stared into his eyes. "Who do you think caused you this pain?"

Michael swallowed, wiping the tears from his eyes. "My dad and uncle did."

Jenny glanced at Grace. The emotions she was feeling had twisted her face, causing her mouth to fall slightly open. Tears were beginning to stream down her face as she remembered her brother tied to that bed of sorrows. Jenny spoke to her in a soft voice. "Grace, if you're hurting and you need to leave, you can."

Grace looked slowly at her and swallowed. "No…no matter what pain I'm in, I'm going to stay with my brother. I love him and I'm not going to leave him now like I left him alone for the past twenty years. We're going through this together."

Jenny looked at Michael again, realizing that he was getting in touch with the real cause of his pain. "Michael, what do you think they did to you in that room?"

Michael began to shift around uneasily on the bench seat. He kept looking around like he was searching for a way to run from the pain he was in. "I don't know! It hurts too much to remember!"

Jenny closed her eyes for a moment before continuing. "I'll tell you what they did. They tied you to that old bed with clotheslines and took off your clothes except for your T-shirt. Then they forced themselves into your ten-year-old body, leaving you there in pain until your sister found you."

Michael gasped and clutched at his pajama top with both his hands as if he were trying to tear it off. The truth she spoke pierced the protective shield he placed around his thoughts like a shard of glass. "Why, those bastards! They used me like I was nothing but a thing to them!" He looked at Jenny as if her face held the answers to the pain he was in.

Jenny looked at him. "Yes, they sexually abused you; they wounded you and took away something very precious…your trust in them." Jenny sighed, speaking to Michael in a soft voice. "Michael…take a deep breath and breathe slowly, in and out. You're okay; you've started to face the things you've been avoiding all these years. I know it's going to be a long process and it's going to be hard at times to deal with hurtful memories, but I'll be here to help you through it all."

She turned to Grace. "Grace, you're a good sister and a wonderful person. I'm proud of you for loving Michael enough to stay by his side." She reached out, squeezing his, then his sister's hands. Then she got up and walked out of the room, taking the files she had on the kitchen table with her. Michael started breathing the way Jenny had told him to do. Then he turned and looked at Grace. They wrapped their arms around each other and broke out crying; their pain flowing out with the tears.

Jenny climbed the back stairs as fast as she could and walked down the upstairs hall into the bedroom she slept in. Dropping her briefcase with the files in it on the floor, she walked over and grabbed a handful of tissues off the dresser. She was determined to help them both. But sometimes she couldn't help but share the pain those two were going through. She sat quietly on her bed with tears streaming slowly down her face.

Down in the family room, Cindy and Chris were reading when they heard Michael and Grace crying. Saying nothing, they laid down their books, got up and walked down the hallway into the kitchen. Cindy sat down next to Michael and wrapped her arms around him, leaning her head on his back. Chris sat down next to Grace, gently holding on to her arm and laying her head on her shoulder.

We Are Like A Living, Breathing Relationship

"You can't forgive what you refuse to remember, any more than you can seek treatment for a disease whose symptoms you have yet to notice."

Carol Luebering - Finding A Way To Forgive (article, CareNotes)

The next morning the sun rose over the inland lake. It warmed the meadow grasses and woke up the birds. A soft breeze blew across the meadow. It rustled the leaves in the trees that stood around the house, then plied its way through the open bedroom windows, causing the curtains to move in and out, like the rooms were breathing on their own. Slowly opening her eyes, Cindy smiled, taking in a deep breath of this early morning freshness. She looked over at Michael who was still asleep. She bent over slowly, kissing him, and then slid out of bed, putting on her bathrobe and slippers.

Walking quietly out of the bedroom, she walked across the hall to the bathroom, turning on its lights. She filled the sink with warm water to wash her face and smiled, thinking it would be a good day to be quiet and comfortable. When she finished, she dried her face and walked out of the bathroom to the bedroom where Grace was sleeping, quietly opening the door. Seeing that Grace was already up, she closed it and walked downstairs.

Stepping into the kitchen, she found Grace already there. "Grace Jacobson! You are a guest here. You don't have to make breakfast."

Grace turned away from the stove and smiled. "Cindy Jacobson, I used to live here, remember?" She looked around the kitchen. "Things may have changed a little but I think I know my way around."

Cindy walked over to the refrigerator and looked in. "Since you're doing the eggs and bacon, why don't I make some oatmeal and squeeze some oranges for juice?"

Grace looked at her. "That sounds good to me. Once you get that done you'd better go wake up the others." Then she sighed. "I'm sorry; here I am bossing you around your own kitchen like it was mine. Please forgive me."

Cindy walked over and gave her a big hug. "Of course you're forgiven. I'm sure I do enough bossing of my own around here." Then she smiled. "Besides, it doesn't hurt for me to take a few orders myself now and then."

Later when breakfast was ready, Cindy looked at the old regulator clock on the wall. She walked over to the back stairs and started climbing. When she reached the second-floor landing, she saw Michael, Chris, and Jenny coming down the hallway in her direction.

Cindy smiled. "Well, I can see the cooking smells woke all three of you up faster than I could." Still smiling, she turned, going back down the back stairs with the three of them right behind her.

During breakfast, Jenny suddenly stopped eating and looked at Michael. "How did you sleep last night?"

"Better than I have in the past month or so." Then he sighed. "Jenny, I have been avoiding my hurt by burying it inside; I'm glad you did what you did yesterday for Grace and me."

Jenny spoke. "I'm glad I did. You need to start facing your hurt, Michael." Then she glanced at her wristwatch. "After breakfast I'm going home to check on Dan and the girls, then I'll be right back."

Breakfast was over and Jenny had left to go home. Michael and Grace decided to take a walk down the old logging road. They hadn't gone far when they found an old fallen tree. Michael unfolded the blanket he was carrying, laying it on the tree's trunk for Grace and him to sit on. After they sat down, Grace looked to the west where the Great Lake bordered the property, north to the forest and inland lake where the old mill sat, south where the house and hangar sat, then east where the busy little town of Crandon was located.

She smiled as she remembered her childhood days, walking alone in the meadow that separated the runway from the forest, lying in the soft meadow grasses mixed with wildflowers. She looked over at her brother, who had picked up a slender stick and was using it to parry with a big beetle. Grace smiled at him. "Still playing with bugs, I see." Smiling, Michael threw away the stick, turned, and looked at her. "We spent a lot of time playing in this meadow, didn't we?"

Grace sighed, then giggled. "Yes, and I loved every minute of it. Speaking of things that hop and crawl, do you remember the time you put a frog in my soup?"

Michael laughed. "Your face turned as green as the frog. You screamed, throwing your bowl with the frog in it across the kitchen. Mom and Dad looked at you, then their soup, and pushed their bowls away."

He smiled, looking into his sister's eyes. "You were always there for me. When I was abused, you became more of a friend to me than you will ever know. How do I ever thank you?"

Grace kissed him on the cheek. "Being your sister is thanks enough. Now, let's get back to the house and I'll make you Grandma Rachael's version of chicken and dumplings for dinner." They walked back to the house with their arms around each other's waists.

It was dinnertime when Jenny parked her SUV behind Grace's car. She picked up her laptop computer, got out of her vehicle, and walked to the back door of the house. Jenny quietly opened the back door, put her computer on a chair nearby, and closed the door. She leaned against it with her arms folded in front of her. She smiled at Michael, Chris, Cindy, and Grace as they moved around each other, helping to make dinner, laughing and poking fun at each other. Suddenly Jenny cleared her throat, causing all four of them to look at her at the same time.

Chris smiled. "You're timing is perfect, Jenny. Here we do all the work getting dinner ready and you show up just in time to eat it." Chris stuck her tongue out at her with Jenny making a face back at her.

"Hey, I had to spend some quality time with my family. But where I am right now is home to me too."

Later, after dinner, everyone was sitting around the table talking. Jenny looked at Michael and touched his arm. "Michael, what were your mom and dad like?"

Michael stared at her for a moment, gathering his thoughts. "Well, they were real active in the church and community. My mom loved to paint. I think some of her paintings are still in the attic. She was a great cook and a good mom and took good care of Grace and me. That is, until I was abused."

She shifted in her chair. "What about your dad?"

Michael struggled a bit before answering. "He taught me some things about flying and he left me the plane and the house we have, if that's any merit."

Jenny looked him in the eyes. "Speaking of merit, let me refresh your memory. I did some research on your dad and uncle, finding out some interesting things about those two." She read from some papers she had just pulled out of her briefcase. "Your dad was a pilot during the Korean War.

He flew an F-86 fighter jet and was responsible for shooting down over ten of the enemy's planes before he was shot down over the demilitarized zone and captured. He escaped through enemy lines, resuming his duties as a pilot before coming home and resigning from the U.S. Air Force.

"He was a highly decorated officer, well respected by his fellow officers. He was often heard to say that he couldn't wait to get home and marry his high school sweetheart and raise a family. Your uncle Dick was a tank commander in Korea, also highly decorated. His tank unit was involved in some of the fiercest firefights in the Korean War. He was awarded the Purple Heart for saving the lives of another tank crew when their tank was disabled. He placed his tank in front of theirs, allowing them to escape unharmed.

"He was wounded as a result, but resumed his duties as soon as he recovered. In his spare time he helped out at a local orphanage, feeding the children with food he had collected." She sighed. "Do they sound like monsters to you?"

Michael looked at her. "No, they don't, but why are you telling me this? I mean, lots of guys served in Korea and probably did what they did. Is there something here that I'm missing?"

"What you don't know is that they both suffered from what we know now as posttraumatic stress disorder as a result of the Korean War. According to your Grandma Rachael and her sister Catherine, they were also abused as boys by their father and uncle, the same way you were abused by yours."

The other women stopped talking and looked at Michael and Jenny. Michael looked at her. "Did that give them a reason to do what they did to me?"

"No, what they did to you was very hurtful and traumatic. You have every reason to be angry, right along with the responsibility to stop this vicious generational cycle you're in by forgiving them."

Michael started to speak, but she interrupted him. "When you forgive someone that has hurt you, you give up your right to judge them regardless of what was done to you. When you don't forgive them, you give evil the legal right to keep you trapped and wounded. As a result, you leave God out and continue to hurt others."

Michael looked at her, frowning. "Whoa! You're talking about spiritual things that are way over my head. Besides, I can't relate to God, Jenny! I don't know how and I can't find a way!"

Jenny sighed deeply. "Go on Michael…I'm listening."

"I have a gut feeling you're going to tell me that God through his spirit is like the wind. You can't see him but you can see how he affects things in our everyday lives. That's great, but I can't relate to the wind! It has no face, no body. It can't respond to you. You can't hold it in your arms, and it can't give you suggestions on how to solve problems.

"Jenny, I go to church practically every Sunday unless I have to work. I've talked to people there who can't relate to God either. They go to church Sunday after Sunday, just like their parents and their parents before them. They go through the ritual without the relationship. They sing songs and listen to the pastor tell them how wonderful God is, how he wants to be a father to them." He sighed and continued. "I've seen hundreds of people in this messed up world that haven't a clue how to relate to God, including me. That leaves them open for any cheap but dangerous lie that dirt bag of a devil wants to throw at them.

"Besides, where was God when that so-called father and uncle of mine used me like a prostitute? Where was he? You tell me!"

Jenny sighed, shaking her head. "Michael, there is no easy answer to that. But what knowledge I have of God tells me that he was in that room grieving over what they were doing to you and sharing your hurt right along with you." Michael glared back at her. "I don't believe you! Why would a loving God let two drunken idiots use a ten-year-old boy like they used me! Why didn't he stop them if he was in that room like you said he was?"

Jenny paused, rubbing her closed eyes and the bridge of her nose with the thumb and forefinger of her right hand. She looked at him, speaking in a firm but soft voice. "God gave us the ability to choose between right and wrong, good and evil. It's not his fault if people are selfish and choose to do evil instead of good. He is not responsible for the choices we make, we are.

"The choices that those two men made that night not only ruined their own lives, they also ruined yours. Because they wouldn't let go of their own pain and forgive their own father and uncle for hurting them, they passed that same pain on by hurting you.

"Now you are alive and they are dead. Everything they said or did ended at the grave. But the spiritual, mental, and emotional residuals of what they said or did comes straight down the spiritual and physical bloodlines of your family, right to you, whether you want them or not. Now it's your choice. Do you want to carry all that hurt and pain around with you the rest of your life? Not only that, do you want your family and friends who love you suffer because they know you're hurting?"

Michael looked at her with the rage slowly dissipating out of his eyes. He hung his head for a moment, then looked up at her. "Jenny, it's hard for me to let go of the hate I have for my father and uncle. I know I don't like what it is doing to me, and I definitely don't like what it is doing to my family. It's not going to be easy to let go of everything they did to me."

Jenny let out a long sigh. "I didn't say it was. I know it's going to be a long process, and I know it's going to hurt for you to bring up the painful memories, let alone deal with them. It's also going to be a waste of your time and mine if you don't forgive your father and uncle for what they did to you. Those three little words--'I forgive you'--spoken out loud, can make the road to healing a whole lot smoother."

There was a long silence as Michael looked out one of the kitchen windows toward the old hangar. After a while he looked back at Jenny. "So, you still think God was in that room with me?" Jenny smiled. "Yes, I do. I also believe that he wanted to prove that he was there when he sent Grace to look for you that night. He was there when your mother washed you up and hugged you, trying to ease your pain. He continued to be with you through the years when you met me, then Cindy. Michael, I believe God relates to us through each other because that's the way he wants it to be. It's God's compassion, not our interpretation of it, that teaches us to love each other regardless of individual faults or differences. It's through his compassionate love that old hurts can be healed, especially when we forgive the ones who hurt us, making a place in us for that love to grow.

"The problem is that people who've been hurt don't always forgive the people that hurt them. They're so wounded they think not forgiving their perpetrators gives them some sort of control over them. It's actually the opposite. The adversary, that dirt bag you mentioned before, has them trapped. He has them exactly where he wants them until they make the choice to forgive.

"Once they forgive or learn to forgive, no trap can hold them anymore, and the healing begins. The amazing thing is that this process often is completed through ordinary people, just like you and me."

Michael looked at her with his head tilted slightly to one side. "Why are you telling me this, Jenny?"

Jenny reached out and took Michael's hand. "We are like a living, breathing relationship, like a human body with all its organs and parts all working together to make life happen. If something is damaged or removed, the whole body suffers. Your family and friends love you more than you know. They hurt when you hurt. Forgive! Break the cycle and give up the hurt that hurts them too."

Michael managed a weak smile. "Then it all comes down to me making the right choices, doesn't it?" Jenny smiled, realizing that the truth was finally getting past his hurt. She squeezed his arm with her hand. "It's getting late. Why don't we go roast some marshmallows over a fire and make s'mores? Besides, I'd love to hear that story of how Teaser, your cat, started the great race."

Later in the evening, when the smoky haze off the burning wood in the fire pit had drifted out over the meadow, and the setting sun was giving way to the first twinkling stars, everyone listened to Cindy give her version of the great race.

She had just licked her fingers from the s'more she had eaten when she giggled. "It was so funny! There I was in curlers with dark green beauty mud all over my face, in our golf cart on the runway, chasing Riley, who was pulling Sarah in her pull cart. Riley was not going to let Teaser get away, and Teaser was not going to let him catch her! The faster they went, the faster I went! Anyway, I was concentrating so much on catching our daughter and our two juvenile delinquent animals, that I didn't notice the wind was blowing the curlers out of my hair, turning it into a fright wig."

The other people around the fire laughed as she continued. "My face was the color of dark green algae. It had just rained, and the water splashing up from the runway off the golf cart's wheels started to soften the beauty mud on my face, making it look like it was melting. So there I was in my fright wig and slimy mud face, trying desperately to catch one four- year-old who was thoroughly enjoying herself and totally ignoring me.

"Then suddenly, out of nowhere, Michael swooped down in his plane landing almost in front of Teaser's nose! He slammed on his brakes, swinging the tail of his plane around with a loud whoosh! It really scared Teaser, and she quickly disappeared into the underbrush nearby. It startled Riley so much that he suddenly sat down on the wet, muddy runway, stopping Sarah and her cart! I was right behind her; I screamed, stomping on the golf cart's brakes to avoid hitting her. That threw me into a skid. I slid by her sideways, yelling and shaking my fist. As I did, she started crying.

"Riley heard Sarah crying and started howling right along with her. I got off the golf cart and stormed over to Sarah and Riley, stomping my feet in the mud and acting more childish than she was. Michael got out of his plane and walked over to us, trying hard not to laugh. He grabbed me around my waist, whispering loving things in my ears until I stopped struggling. When I turned around in his arms, I smiled at him through the green mud sliding off my face. That's when he lost it. He laughed so hard he had to grab ahold of the golf cart to keep from slipping and falling on the muddy runway.

"I glared at him and stomped my feet all the more. Trying to catch his breath, he pointed to the rearview mirror on the golf cart. I looked in it, not knowing if I should laugh, cry, or throw mud.

Michael mentioned I should go hug my crying four-year-old. I wanted to spank her, but ended up picking her out of her cart and hugging her.

"She stopped crying for a while, until she looked up at my face. Then she cried out, 'You aren't my mommy! My mommy isn't green!'

By this time, everyone around the fire was in hysterics.

Cindy continued, "Just then a glob of beauty mud slid off my face into one of her hands. She stopped crying and put some of it into her mouth, immediately spitting it out. Then she looked up at me, saying, 'Your face tastes awful!' She was right; it tasted terrible to me too.

"Michael pulled out a camera he had and took a picture of us. It sits on our mantel in the family room, and that's the story of the great race."

Cindy joined in the laughter, then got up helping pick up the leftover food. As Cindy, Chris, and Grace were walking back to the house, Michael put out the fire with a bucket of water, not noticing that Jenny was standing there watching him. As soon as the fire was out, he set the empty bucket down, looking up from the kneeling position he was in. He saw her smiling at him. "Whenever you smile like that, it means you can't wait to share something with me."

Jenny stopped smiling and got serious. "Michael, not forgiving someone is like clenching your fist around a handful of broken glass. It not only causes you pain, but it keeps on wounding you, until one day you get to the point where you wonder why you held on to it in the first place."

Michael looked down at the ground and back up at her. "You haven't gone through what I have. You don't know what it's like; how hard it is to forgive my dad and uncle for what they did to me!"

Jenny sighed. "You're right; I haven't gone through the same thing that you have, but I did lose my parents when I was younger. I had a hard time forgiving the drunk driver involved in the accident that killed them, or forgiving God for not intervening. I was so hurt and confused that living became a burden. Then this wonderful man bumped into me in a college cafeteria one day, knocking my tray of food out of my hands. I got to know him, immediately spilling out all my pain from the loss of my parents. He stopped whatever he was doing just to make time for me. The compassion he shared with me changed my heart. It taught me how to forgive God and the drunk driver. I'll never forget the selfless love he gave me."

Michael stood up and hugged her. "I couldn't have shared it with a better friend. Now let's go back to the house. Tomorrow I give my daughter her first flying lesson in my plane." Then he smiled. "Regardless of how much she thinks she knows about flying."

Time For Grace

"Sometimes forgiving was easy for me; sometimes forgiving was a very bold choice. Whatever kind of choice it was, it always led me to a more peaceful heart. It always left me happier and free to move on to create healthier relationships with others and with myself."

Robin Casarjian - *Forgiveness: A Bold Choice For A Peaceful Heart*

It was early the next morning after breakfast, and Michael and Chris had just taken off in his plane. Grace and Jenny were in the kitchen cleaning up the dishes, and Cindy was in her craft room doing some inventory on her craft supplies. Jenny looked up from the sink at Grace wiping off the kitchen table with a damp sponge. "Do you think you could talk your brother into buying a dishwasher? It sure would save us time."

Grace looked up at her, smiling. "You're right; I think he should. Just because there are three women in the house doesn't mean we have to be stuck with doing dishes all the time."

Jenny rinsed the last of the dishes, placing them in the rack to dry. "Grace, there is something I've wanted to talk to you about."

As they sat down in the nook with their coffee cups, Jenny shared what she was thinking. "You told me a little about your childhood at my office when I met you for the first time. What was it like when you were growing up?"

Grace looked around the kitchen and back at her. "Our parents were great. They didn't argue about things; they discussed them most of the time, coming to a mutual agreement. My father never yelled at my mother, and she never complained about everyday matters to him. She was a good mother who honored her husband. They loved us and provided for us.

I thought it would go on forever."

Then she sighed. "When Michael was abused, the life we knew came to a very emotional halt. You can imagine the shock I went through when I found my brother in that room upstairs. My trust in my father and uncle was destroyed, right along with my brother's. It was like a heavy blanket had been thrown over our family, and all of us were struggling to breathe. My father still provided for us all, but he had changed so much. It was a scene right out of Jekyll and Hyde. I confronted my father several times about what he and Uncle Dick did to Michael, and he denied it every time. He said he couldn't even remember doing anything to my brother, and was wondering why Michael was acting the way he was to him and Uncle Dick. Now I know why. He and my uncle were not dealing with their own hurt and drank to avoid dealing with it." She paused, then continued. "Whenever they would drink, Michael and I would run to the old mill and hide. We had our own supply of blankets and canned food there in case we had to stay overnight. Our father and uncle would get drunk sometimes two or three times a month, so we got used to going there. When winter came we would hide in the cellar. Michael and I had made a space behind some old cabinets that were used to store canned goods. We would wrap up in some old blankets and sleep sitting up near each other just to keep warm. I had a baseball bat across my lap if those two came down there, but they never did. Michael and I lived like this for two years until he turned twelve. Then my dad and uncle got killed in a hunting accident. I was sad, but in a way relieved."

She took a sip of coffee and continued. "Later when Michael had just turned sixteen, he and I made plans to leave here. One night we packed our suitcases and left."

Jenny shook her head. "Just like that, without saying good-bye or leaving a note. Without any regard or thought to what your mother had gone through or how she was hurting!"

Grace stared back at her in defiance. "She had Aunt Ruth! Are you trying to make me feel guilty, Jenny?"

Jenny sighed. "I am not trying to make you feel guilty; I am trying to help you see things from a different perspective. Up until the time your brother was abused, you had a great family; much more than a lot of children have. Grace, we are talking about your mother who, along with your father, brought you and Michael into this world. She's the one who nursed you, dressed and fed you, and stayed up all night with you when you were sick. She wiped your runny noses, bathed you, and held you when you were afraid. Was she a throwaway mom or a nanny that just did her job and that's all?"

Jenny paused for a moment to give time for her words to sink in. "Try to visualize this scenario. Let's say you and Michael take Sarah with you one day to go shopping. Sarah is sitting in the cart, and Michael is somewhere else in the store. You leave her for just a minute, walking back down the aisle because you forgot something. When you turn around to go back to the cart, Sarah is gone. You leave your cart and start looking down all the aisles in the store, but you can't find her. Starting to panic, you rush up to the front of the store, where you find the manager and tell him your niece is missing. He calls the police, and when they arrive you tell them your story and they get a picture of Sarah from you, along with your contact information.

"Now you and Michael go home, and you worry and pray that nothing has happened to her. You don't sleep; you hardly eat, knowing someone has abducted her. Then you get the phone call. The police have found her, and she has been physically molested. You go into shock and have a near nervous breakdown, not able to forgive yourself for not keeping all this from happening. Does this describe how you would've reacted?"

Grace exhaled slowly. "Yes, exactly how I would have reacted."

Jenny looked in her eyes. "Now you have a good idea what your mother went through with

Michael. Grace, please remember this is not just about your brother and you."

There was a long silence as Grace hung her head. Then she raised it slowly, looking at Jenny with tears in her eyes. "You're right. We were thinking about ourselves and not about our mother, or how this whole thing would affect her."

Grace sighed, wiping the tears from her eyes with her hands. "After we left, we hitchhiked down to Manchester, staying with our Grandma Rachael and her sister. Our mother found out where we were and called repeatedly, begging us to come home. But we ignored her. Grandma Rachael tried to convince us that we should go back home to our mother, but we were stubborn and didn't listen to her. Not too long after that, our Aunt Ruth called, saying that our mother had died. After that, Aunt Ruth went to live with her sister until she died. At our mother's funeral, we finally realized how foolish and selfish we were in leaving her. After we buried her next to our father, we closed up the house and went our separate ways.

"Michael worked in a factory until he saved enough money to go to college, and I got a job as a waitress, using the money I earned to pay my way through business school. I graduated, starting my own interior decorating business. I recently sold it, paying off the mortgage on my house. The rest I set aside for an emergency fund.

"Then out of the blue I decided to call Michael. I was starting to have some recurring nightmares about the night I found him tied to that bed. I was also ashamed for not keeping in contact with him.

That's when I called Cindy. Then I met you and decided to sell my house and move in here. It's been a big decision for me, but I love my brother and his family and want to be close to them. Besides, it's given me the family of my own that I never had."

Jenny smiled. "Don't you want children of your own?"

Grace smiled at her. "I'm a year older than Michael. I can't have children at my age. Besides, I've been single for so long. I haven't had any thoughts about marriage until I met Dave just recently." She giggled. "Maybe I do have a few hormones left alive in me."

Grace looked at Jenny for a moment, then smiled. "Jenny, come with me; I have some things I want to show you."

Together they walked out of the kitchen, climbing to the second floor. They walked toward the attic door, stopping in front of it. Grace took the key for the attic door off its hook, glancing at her parents' bedroom. The ugliness was gone and its freshness warmed her, like the sunlight pouring through its opened windows.

Grace smiled at Jenny. "I like my new bedroom. I know I could have chosen another room after I moved in, but after all the work you girls did on it, I wasn't about to let fear or any bad memory keep me from it. But that's not what I want to show you." Grace opened the attic door, turning on an old light switch. Cobweb-covered lights lit the staircase leading to a trove of family memories. Grace and Jenny climbed the narrow stairs. When they reached the top landing, she stopped, turning on another set of lights that illuminated the whole attic area.

Jenny noticed that Grace's eyes were starting to tear up. She put her arm around her shoulder. "Is there anything I can help you with, Grace?"

Grace sighed. "It's just that every time I come up here, I can imagine all my family, from Isaac and Isabelle Jacobson to my own parents, standing here and staring right back at me. Sometimes I think I should just throw or give most of these things away. But they're also the only ties that I have with my past." Jenny looked around the attic and back at Grace. "Grace, the connections with our ancestors goes deeper than what they leave behind. They also left us their looks, their talents, and the generational impact of what they said or did, whether it was good or bad. We can enjoy the good, but the problem is we sometimes bury the bad, refusing to face and deal with it. It's like a cork that you attach a weight to and throw in a lake. Sooner or later it will pop to the surface, fly out, and hit you right in your face." Grace understood Jenny's point. "You're right, Jenny; Michael and I have been doing that too long and it has to stop."

Grace walked over to an old steamer trunk, slowly lifting the lid. "Why don't we start here?"

Jenny walked over, kneeling beside her on the attic floor. She looked in the trunk with her. "May I?"

Grace smiled, nodding her head. Jenny picked up two old photographs that were encased in glass-covered picture frames. She studied the faces in the photographs that stared back at her. It looked like they were trying to say something, but couldn't because their words had been frozen in time. Then she carefully laid them on the floor next to her, picking up an old rag doll. Sighing, she laid the doll down, pulling out a dried, faded rose wrapped in tissue paper and tied with a ribbon. A handwritten paper note attached to it read, "To my darling wife Isabelle from her husband Isaac on our twenty-fifth wedding anniversary."

Jenny smiled. "They must have been deeply in love for him to give her this rose, and for her to keep it all those years."

Grace fingered the timeworn note and smiled. "Grandma Rachael said she remembered when she was a girl how affectionate they were to each other, even in their old age."

Jenny carefully laid the rose down, looking at the vast array of items in the attic. "Grace, it's going to take a long time to go through all this."

Grace smiled. "I know. That's why I suggested we start with this trunk. There are some letters in here that I think you need to read. You're welcome to read them in private. I'm going down to start lunch for all of us. Michael and Chris will be back soon, and you know how hungry he gets."

Jenny smiled at her as she disappeared down the attic stairs. Then she reached into the trunk, talking to herself. She pulled out several packets of old letters tied with string that had turned brown with age.

"I can see this is going to take longer than I thought, but I'll do anything to find out where the family patterns of abuse started."

Grace was in the kitchen taking food out of the the refrigerator when Cindy walked in from her craft room, looking at a pad full of items she needed. She looked at Grace and smiled. "Where's Jenny?"

"She's up in the attic going through a few things." Cindy laughed. "Do you realize that leaving her up there is like leaving a lady who craves sweets all alone in a bakery?"

Grace laughed. "I know, but if she wants to get to know my family, that's the best place to start."

Lunch was soon ready and set on the table. As Grace was pouring some freshly made lemonade, the back door opened and in walked Michael and Chris. Michael smiled and walked over, kissing Cindy. "As usual, you two were anticipating my appetite."

Chris put her hands on her hips. "Just a minute, Sky King. I have an appetite too and you, you put me through the wringer up there. Turn here, turn there, push that, switch on those. 'Hey! Watch what you're doing with my plane, it doesn't trim trees too well!' You got me really stressed out for a minute up there. I'm so hungry I could eat half your airplane." Then she stuck her tongue out at him.

Michael walked over, hugged her, then held her at arm's length. "Chris, you're a great pilot. If you can take all the things I threw at you in the short time we were in the air, still flying the way you did, I'll gladly give you an extra set of keys to my plane. You can take it up anytime you want. As far as I'm concerned, that plane out there is half yours."

Michael walked over to the sink and started to

wash his hands. Chris stood there with her hands still on her hips and her mouth slightly open, trying to absorb what he had said. Cindy stared at Chris for a minute, then walked over to her and whispered in her ear. "Go give your father a hug and tell him that you love him…now!"

Chris ran over and hugged her dad, looking up at him with a big smile on her face. "I love you, Dad. Don't you ever forget that!"

Michael smiled at her. "I won't. Now let's eat, because the next lesson for today is aircraft servicing and maintenance 101, which I can guarantee will ruin those beautiful fingernails of yours."

Chris looked at her fingernails, then made a face, joining him at the table. As they were eating, Grace suddenly got a strange look on her face. Cindy looked at her. "Are you okay, Grace?"

"I just remembered-- I left Jenny up in the attic and forgot to tell her that lunch was ready."

Cindy smiled as she threw her hands up in mock fright. "We have to get her out of there before she suffers a severe attack of information overload! Chris, you'd better go rescue her. No doubt she has herself surrounded by huge piles of everything, and can't find her way out!"

The group at the table was laughing as Jenny came walking slowly down the back staircase into the kitchen. Everyone stopped laughing and looked at her staring at them with a wide-eyed look on her face. Then they started laughing again.

Jenny finally spoke, "Go ahead! Laugh yourselves silly at me because I am suffering from brain damage, caused by too much research in that information highway of an attic upstairs!"

Later when all of them were still eating, the phone rang. Grace got up and answered it. She stood there for a moment listening, then smiled broadly. "They did? They accepted my offer? Great! Yes! Have the bank send down the papers and I'll sign them."

Grace hung up the phone. Everyone started cheering and congratulating Grace on the sale of her house. It was a good day for all of them. Little did they know there was a storm building, and it wasn't coming out of the northwest. It would hit the Jacobson homestead without warning sometime after eight o'clock the following morning.

The Hidden Storm

"Forgiving does not erase the bitter past. A healed memory is not a deleted memory. Instead, forgiving what we cannot forget creates a new way to remember. We change the memory of our past into a hope for our future."

Beverly Flanigan - Forgiving The Unforgivable: Overcoming the Legacy of Intimate Wounds

At precisely 8:45 a.m. the next morning, Michael and Chris took off in his plane. They were headed to the mainland where Michael would introduce his daughter to all his business acquaintances and the new postmistress. Jenny and Cindy were sitting in the nook talking. Grace was raising one of the window shades in the kitchen when she saw a strange car pull up and stop next to Jenny's SUV. Curious, she opened the back door, coming face to face with the young woman about to knock on it.

Both women stood there looking at each other for a moment, then their eyes widened and both gasped at once. The younger woman started shaking. "I have to leave; I knew I shouldn't have come here! I'm so sorry!"

Grace was startled. The young woman's resemblance to hers was amazing. She gently took hold of one of her arms, not letting her get away. "Please come in. I'm sure there has to be an explanation to all of this."

The young woman walked into the kitchen. Grace closed the back door and stood next to her. Cindy and Jenny stopped talking, got up from the table, and walked over to them.

After a few awkward moments, Jenny smiled. "I'm Jenny Peterson. My husband and I are friends to Michael. This is his wife, Cindy, and his sister, Grace."

Still trembling, the young woman managed to smile. "I want to thank you all for inviting me in. You don't know how much courage it took just for me to come out here."

Cindy put her arm around her shoulder and walked her over to the kitchen table, pulling out a chair for her. Grace inquired, "Would you like something to drink?"

"Yes, I would. Just a glass of water with some ice in it would be fine." Grace brought her the water and sat down opposite her at the table with Jenny and Cindy. The young woman looked around at everyone, then cleared her throat and sighed.

"My name is Melissa Jacobson and…"

Grace was suspicious. "Who did you say you were?"

Melissa closed her eyes for a moment, then opened them. "Please let me explain."

Grace folded her arms in front of her. "Yes, please do!"

"I lived until recently in Cadillac, attending a business college there. After I graduated, I worked as a certified public accountant for a large corporation in the area. Unfortunately, the company downsized, laying me off. I saw an ad in a paper mentioning a CPA position here in Crandon at a cement and gravel company. I came back here to the island, applied for the job, and got it.

"In my spare time I make extra money working in the city courthouse retyping and updating old records. I was working on the 'J' section recently when I came across several birth records with my last name. There was one with your name, Grace, and one with your brother's. On your records the parents' names were Shelly and Roger Jacobson.

"For some reason, probably curiosity, I dug deeper in the back of that file cabinet until I found an old manila envelope marked 'Adoption papers for M. Jacobson.' I opened the envelope and read the adoption forms. Here, look at these copies I made for you."

Grace's hands started shaking as she read. Laying the papers down, she stared at Melissa. "This isn't true. It can't be true!"

Melissa sighed. "Is this your mother's signature?" Grace nodded. "Then I guess it is. Along with the adoption forms, but in a separate, sealed envelope, were forms that included the names of my birth parents, Roger Jacobson and Evelyn Thompson. Your mother couldn't have known who my real parents were because she wasn't told who they were. I didn't know until now. I was six when your mother and aunt took me out of the foster home I was in. I lived here in this house for twelve years; when your mother died I went to live with your aunt for three years until she died. I was twenty-one when I went to college. I'm sorry it's a shock to you, Grace, but these other papers with my birth parents names on them, tell me that I'm your half sister."

Grace was having a hard time with Melissa. Why did she have to show up when her own life was in so much turmoil? Just then the sound of Michael's airplane was heard in the distance.

Cindy looked at Melissa. "That will be Michael and Chris coming back from the mainland. He and Chris have no idea who you are and why you came. You owe them an explanation, Melissa."

Soon Michael and Chris came walking in the back door. When they spotted Melissa sitting at the table, they stopped and looked at her.

Michael smiled. "You know, Grace, if I didn't think I was seeing double, I'd swear that you have a new sister."

Chris smiled. "I agree. You two look exactly alike."

Grace finally conceded, accepting Melissa for who she was. "Michael, say hello to your new half sister. Apparently Mother and Aunt Ruth kept her a secret from us. She showed up at our back door this morning."

When Michael and Chris sat down, Melissa extended her right hand and shook his hand. "Hello, Michael, I'm so glad to meet you."

Michael didn't quite know what to make of her. "I can't get over the fact that you look just like my sister did when she was around twenty-five."

Just then Grace cleared her throat, making a face at him. Michael looked at her, trying hard to backpedal himself out of his last statement. "Uh, Grace, you always look like you're twenty-five… and holding."

Grace smiled. "I think you'd better quit while you're still ahead!"

Michael cleared his throat. "So, you were about to explain how you became a part of our family… right?"

Melissa sighed. "I think you had better look at this first."

She handed him the adoption papers that Grace had read earlier. Michael read through them until he came to the part that listed the names of her birth parents. Suddenly the expression on his face changed. "My father was your father? I don't believe it!"

Melissa looked at him. "Michael, I couldn't accept it either when I found out. Your mother didn't know her husband had an affair with a high school math teacher. I didn't know it, and your mother never told me what really happened to your father and my father. When I was living here, I would often look at pictures of you and your sister on the wall of her bedroom. Once I found her crying and holding a picture of you two. I put my arm around her shoulders, asking if there was anything I could do, and she cried saying there wasn't. She said she still loved you two, hoping you would forgive her for not being the mother she should have been. I was eighteen the day she died. She looked at me from the bed she was in, so weak she could barely smile. She told me she loved me like her daughter. I started to cry and knelt beside her bed, asking her if she was ready to meet God. She said she was. I told her that there was no one that could have loved me more than she had. A few minutes later she looked at me and smiled. Then she closed her eyes for the last time. I went downstairs and told Aunt Ruth what happened. She dropped what she was doing and ran upstairs. Later I walked over to the bottom of the stairs and listened.

"I heard her crying and talking to someone on the phone in the bedroom. Then she came down the stairs, wiping her eyes, saying she was taking me to her sister's house. Your aunt helped me pack. That's the last time I saw your mother and this house. I lived with Aunt Ruth and her sister for three years, turning twenty-one the day she died. It was a cold, dismal October day. I was in her bedroom taking care of her because she was sick in bed. I had just put an ice pack on her head when she grabbed my hand.

"As I sat down on the edge of her bed she told me something that I have never forgotten to this day."

Then Melissa told the story of how Shelly was so emotionally hurt that she had convinced herself that Melissa was her own daughter, Grace. Melissa paused, wiping the tears from her eyes. "How do you think that made me feel, that I wasn't wanted by my birth mother or father, and the woman who adopted me made me into the daughter that had left her?"

She was quiet for a moment. "After I graduated from college and got the job on the mainland, I lived day to day in an emotional fog. I had to shut my emotions down just so I could survive. When I got the job here on the island, I didn't know that I'd find myself back here at this house.

I realize that I have no right to ask you this, but you two are the only family I have left in this world. Is there any way you'd let me be part of it?"

Michael looked at his half sister, not saying a word. He stood up, pulling her out of her chair by her shoulders, and held her in his arms. Melissa wrapped her arms around her brother. Michael knew that she had found a place in his heart.

After a short while, Grace smiled and broke the silence. "Melissa, as far as I'm concerned, don't ever let anyone tell you that you aren't part of this family. Now I want to hear everything about you, and every day you spent here, right, Michael?"

Michael let go of his newfound sister. "Sure, why not. Before I had only one sister to pick on. Now I have two."

Everyone laughed as Grace stood up, playfully shoving him. Melissa knew she had finally found a home. Not just one made of wood and bricks, but a home in the hearts of a wonderful family that would learn to love her just as much as her own mother should have. The hidden storm was over, and a sister had came back home.

Don't Let The Darkness Hide

"Forgiveness is a rebirth of hope, a reorganization of thought, and a reconstruction of dreams. Once forgiving begins, dreams can be rebuilt. When forgiving is complete, meaning has been extracted from the worst of experiences and used to create a new set of moral rules and a new interpretation of life's events."

Beverly Flanigan - Forgiving The Unforgivable: Overcoming the Legacy of Intimate Wounds

Everyone sat back down at the kitchen table, listening as Melissa shared about her life. As she talked, Michael began to notice how much Melissa reminded him of his father. She had his eyes, and every time she looked at him, he could see his father looking back at him. He knew that was impossible, but it still bothered him.

Over time Melissa became a welcome sight around the old home. When she visited, she always brought something with her. Usually it was that wonderful smile she had, but other times it was muffins or plants and flowers or craft material that she thought Cindy could use.

The month of June had passed. The Jacobson family was preparing for a Fourth of July picnic for themselves and their friends.

Michael and Chris had just taken off in the plane for the mainland, and Melissa was there helping prepare food with Grace and Cindy. Melissa had just put plastic wrap over a bowl of mixed fruit when Jenny walked in the back door. She looked at Grace. "Well, it looks as though I came just in time to get my hands dirty. Have you got something I can do?"

Grace handed her a bag of vegetables and a knife. Jenny took the bag over to the sink to wash and cut them up. Later in the afternoon when most of the food was prepared, the women sat down at the table to talk.

Suddenly Jenny spoke up. "Since Melissa's part of the family, don't you think she should know what's going on with Michael? After all, he is her brother."

Melissa looked at Cindy. then at Grace. "What about my brother?"

Grace explained. "When Michael was ten years old, he was sexually abused by his father and uncle, the husband of Aunt Ruth, in the bedroom that used to belong to our parents. I didn't want to tell you right away because he hasn't been having the nightmares, or flashbacks related to the trauma he's been through." She paused for a moment. "It's not going to be easy watching our brother go through what he has to go through. If you stick with us, you'll have to share the bad times as well as the good. It's up to you."

Melissa's mind was made up. "Grace, there's no other place I'd rather be." Then she sighed, remembering a part of her past. "When I was living here, I sometimes would hear your mother talking in her sleep. She would say the same things over and over. Things like, 'I should have stayed with my son that night.' or 'Michael, Michael, why did they have to do that to you?' Sometimes she would call out your name, Grace, asking for your help. Some nights she would cry herself to sleep.

"All the time I lived here I wanted so much to ease the pain she was in, but I couldn't. I loved her the best way I could. I tried to be there whenever she needed me. I tried to make her laugh, and that was hard because she was often depressed. Now I think I know why she was. She was blaming herself for the night Michael was abused. When you two left she blamed herself for not being a good mother.

"What I can't understand is, why didn't you two forgive her?"

Grace tried to explain. "Michael and I were both selfish. We obviously didn't want what she wanted, which was to keep this family together regardless of all the hell we were going through. That's why this family needs to stick together now and help each other through this mess."

Cindy looked over at Melissa. "Melissa, how much are you paying for rent at that condo you live in?"

"About $850 a month, but that includes utilities."

"What would you say if I asked you to live here with us?"

Melissa looked at her for a moment, then spoke. "Well, I would say it's a wonderful idea. On the practical side, it would save me $850 a month in rent, and I could help with the cleaning and cooking. I know I'd make a great babysitter for Sarah and Abby. Chris and I are becoming good friends, so I'd have someone to hang out with. The best part would be living here with all of you. I would finally have a family and a place I could really call my home, and that's a place I have been looking for all my life."

Jenny's mind was elsewhere. "Grace, I think all of us, including Michael, should pay a visit to the graveyard where his parents and grandparents are buried."

Grace was skeptical. "I don't know, Jenny. When we buried our mother next to our father, Michael didn't get out of the car to go to the graveside ceremony. To this day he's never been there, and I don't think you or anyone of us could get him to go, no matter how hard we tried."

Melissa sighed. "I've never been there. Roger was my father too. I know I can't talk with him, but I can at least talk at the tombstone, venting some of my pent-up emotions at the man I never knew."

Jenny was adamant. "You took the words right out of my mouth, Melissa. I think we all need to vent some of our emotions there, especially Michael. He'll probably do more crying and screaming than all of us put together, which will help him get more of his pain out in the open. How about planning on doing it after the holiday? Right now, let's get Melissa settled into her new home and finish up things for the big party on the Fourth."

Melissa was excited. Although she had lived

in the same house as Michael and Grace, it didn't seem like home to her because of the emotional turmoil and lack of a father. She was able to get out of her lease and get her deposit back, and then moved into the bedroom she had occupied as a teenager.

The Fourth of July finally arrived. It came with its usual patriotic fervor and the reminders of the human cost to secure it. With the parades and speeches came the family get-togethers, picnics, and the glorious, thunderous displays of fireworks.

The party at the Jacobson's was no different. In the evening everyone lined themselves up along the runway, sitting down in their lawn chairs and on blankets, all donning insect repellant. Everyone had an excellent view of the fireworks display that was cosponsored by the local Veterans of Foreign Wars and the Lions Club.

The fireworks display lasted for over a half an hour. As the last glorious burst of color lit the sky, everyone cheered and clapped before gathering up their chairs and blankets.

Michael and Cindy sat on their picnic table, watching the last of their friends leave. Michael turned to Cindy and kissed her. Cindy smiled at him. "Thankyou, and I love you too."

Michael wrapped his arms around her. "I know you do. I knew it the day you kissed me in that football stadium." He looked at the last car leaving their driveway. "This was a great Fourth of July celebration, don't you think?"

Cindy looked over at him. "Yes it was, but don't you think we should clean up this mess? The girls and I have something planned for you tomorrow, so we need to get to bed." Michael took the box of garbage bags she handed him, pulled one out, and started to pick up the trash that lay scattered on the ground.

The next morning the sun rose brightly over the back of the old hangar and outbuildings. The shifting wind blew the last few remainders of yesterday's celebration around and around, finally depositing them in the flower beds that surrounded the house. Inside the house, the smells of breakfast cooking filled the air, waking everyone from a good night's sleep. Everyone soon found their way into the kitchen.

Michael looked up from his mug of coffee at Cindy. "You know, sweetheart, I think just about every bedroom in this house is filled up."

Cindy smiled at him. "Isn't it great? It's filled with family, and that's what makes a house a home. By the way, Jenny just called and said she was coming over, so we should get out of our pj's and get dressed."

Michael set his coffee mug down. "She sure has been spending a lot of time at home lately; but I don't blame her, I would too."

"Well, she misses her husband and family a lot, just like I miss Abby and Sarah."

Outside Jenny drove up in her SUV and parked it next to Melissa's car. She sat there for a moment, collecting her thoughts. As she walked up to the back door, she heard classical music coming from Grace's bedroom above her. Stopping, she listened for a moment, recognizing Franz Liszt's Hungarian Rhapsody no#5. It was good to hear music coming out of that room instead of the stark memories of pain and death. Jenny opened the kitchen door, finding everyone except Grace sitting around the table dressed and waiting for her.

Jenny looked at them. "Are we all ready to go?" Everyone went out the back door single file and got into the station wagon in the carport, waiting for Grace to come out. Later, about a half mile from their destination, Cindy pulled the station wagon over to the side of the road.

She looked back at Michael. "Michael please put on this blindfold before we go any farther."

Michael put the blindfold she handed him over his eyes, wondering what she was up to. Shortly after that, Cindy turned the station wagon into Elmwood Memorial Cemetery and stopped it. Everyone got out and followed Michael, who was led by Melissa to his family burial plot. Melissa opened the gate to the iron fence surrounding the graves, leading Michael over to a pair of headstones.

On Jenny's signal, Melissa removed Michael's blindfold, stepping back to where the other women were standing. Michael rubbed his eyes with both hands and looked down at the tombstones in front of him, recognizing the names. He quickly turned around, looking at all the women standing there.

Shaking, Michael buried his face in his hands. "Why did you bring me here? I don't want to be near these people at all!"

Jenny walked up within two feet of him with the other women right behind her. She looked him in the eyes and spoke softly, slowly increasing the volume of her voice. "Michael, these people can't hurt you anymore. In fact, they can't even hear you. Everything they did to you and Grace has ended right here with these graves. It's time you ended it too. Go ahead, shout at them and swear at them and call them every name in the book. Go ahead and kick at these stones and spit on them. Don't let the darkness hide in you anymore!"

Then Jenny stepped back, motioning with her hand for the other women to do the same. Suddenly Michael's face turned red and the veins on his head and neck stood out. He began screaming. All the anguish and pain came out of him at once. His adrenaline was flowing when he rushed to his father's headstone and began to kick it. As Michael was kicking the stone, he yelled out all the hate that he held inside for his father. He called him every filthy name he could think of. Suddenly he lunged at the headstone with both hands, breaking it off its foundation. Then he got up and ran over to his uncle's tombstone, shoving it off its base onto its back. With his hands bloodied from the sharp edges of the broken gravestones, Michael stumbled over, collapsed on his father's fallen headstone, and wept.

Everyone watching him stood there in silence, tears flowing down their faces. Cindy and Grace slowly approached Michael, who was still lying on the headstone crying and sobbing. They knelt down and lifted him off the cold granite headstone into their arms. They didn't care whether or not his blood stained their coats, or that he held on to them so tightly it cut off some of their circulation.

Jenny, along with Chris and Melissa, walked

over and knelt around Cindy, Grace, and Michael. Saying nothing, they all held onto Michael, hoping that what he had just gone through had finally given his heart and mind some desperately needed freedom.

New Beginning

"Forgiving does not usually happen at once. It is a process, sometimes a long one, especially when it comes to wounds gouged deep.

Lewis B. Smedes, Forgive & Forget:
Healing the Hurts We Don't Deserve

Cindy drove the station wagon into the carport and turned off its engine. Sighing, she looked in the rearview mirror at Michael sitting in the seat behind her. His eyes were closed as if he was sleeping. Cindy and Melissa helped him out of the station wagon and up the stairs to the bathroom where Cindy gave him a bath and Melissa bandaged up his hands. The other women hung their coats on the wooden pegs beside the back door, walked over to the chairs in the nook, and collapsed in them.

Chris looked at Jenny and spoke. "You did it again, Jenny."

"I didn't do it; Michael did it. I just got him started in the right direction. Normally I wouldn't have done what I did to him with any of my other clients. I probably would've shown them pictures of some tombstones, letting them take out their vengeance on a pillow instead of the real thing." She paused. "I really took a risk with Michael. I didn't want to take him to the graveyard at first; then I realized that he would probably have felt more secure and safe in my office, and as cruel as it sounds, I didn't want him to feel that way. He needed to do this. He needed to face one of the things he's been running from and avoiding all these years."

Grace spoke up. "I want to thank you too. I don't think you heard me yelling right along with my brother. I ended up kicking over a few urns myself. We made a mess there, but, oh, did it feel good to do it."

Jenny sighed. "I can't take credit for what happened today because this type of exposure therapy has been used before. What I didn't know is how much anger and pain Michael had inside or how much would come out. Maybe I should have handled it another way...but...what's done is done and I'm going home." The next day was Sunday and Jenny suggested that everyone, herself included, get some rest. Then she left.

Chris looked at Grace and smiled. "I think you and Michael really had a breakthrough today."

Grace sighed. "Speaking of breaking things, I can imagine what it's going to cost to fix the mess we made."

Chris stifled a laugh. "Don't worry about it, Grace; we'll find someone to fix the stones."

The next day the sun rose, bathing the forest in light and warmth. An early morning breeze caressed the wildflowers in the meadow, filling every room of the old house with a fresh bouquet of scent. Grace was the first to wake up. She stretched, yawned, and sat up in bed, rubbing her eyes. She walked over to an open window, sitting down in an old rocking chair that once belonged to her mother.

Grace loved this time of the morning when it was almost quiet enough to hear your heart beat. She smiled, taking a deep breath. It felt wonderful to be alive. She reached down and put on her slippers. Then she took her bathrobe off one of the posts of her brass bed. She walked out of her bedroom into the hallway, slipping into her bathrobe, then down the back stairway and into the kitchen. Making breakfast was one of the things she loved to do when she was growing up as a girl, and this morning was no different.

Upstairs, Michael was just waking up to the smells of Grace's cooking, which slowly and tantalizingly wafted up from the kitchen below. As he rolled over to get up, his bandaged hands painfully reminded him of yesterday's fiasco at the cemetery. Michael smiled broadly. The pain in his hands was nothing compared to the peace of mind he had. He felt like he had been given a new beginning.

He looked over at Cindy's sleeping face. She looked so serene and peaceful that he didn't want to wake her. Suddenly she stirred and opened her eyes, looking up. "Good morning, handsome. How do you feel?"

"Other than the pain in my hands I feel terrific. Say, why don't we go pick up our daughters at Jenny's house and go camping on the lake?"

Cindy raised herself up on her elbows and kissed him. "I would love to, sweetheart, but your hands have to heal first. I don't think you could fly your plane, let alone drive a car or go camping. Relax, Chris will do the flying for you and you can take it easy until you heal."

Just then the phone on Cindy's nightstand rang. Cindy answered it pleased at what she heard. "You're kidding! They fixed them already? Yes, I'll tell them both." Hanging up the phone, she looked at Michael. "Jenny told Dan about the tombstones. She said Dan and a couple of guys went right out and fixed them and the urns that Grace kicked over. We have a couple of really sweet friends, you know that?"

"You're right, we do, but I have a hunch that they feel the same way about us." He looked down at his hands. "Who wrapped my hands? Whoever did used way too many bandages."

Cindy made a face at him. "Excuse me, but your half sister did. I gave you a bath and we both put you to bed. You were such a mess yesterday I don't think you even noticed."

"I'm sorry. You're right; I was a mess. Thank you for taking care of me."

Cindy looked at him. "I'm taking you to the hospital today. I am going to have them x-ray your hands. I want to make sure you didn't break anything. How do you feel right now? I mean about what you did at the cemetery."

Michael leaned over, kissing her on the forehead. "I feel better. I know I left a lot of crud there that I'd been carrying around for years. I didn't realize just how much anger had built up in me. I'm glad I took it out on those headstones instead of any of you. I want to thank you and Jenny for doing what you did."

Cindy looked at Michael. She slid out of bed, putting on her slippers and bathrobe. "I'm going downstairs to help Grace with breakfast."

He looked at her. "Cindy, didn't you hear me?"

Cindy stared at him for a moment. "Yes, I did. But what I haven't heard is you forgiving the people that hurt you. It's up to you. Nothing is going to change until you do." Cindy kissed him on his forehead, turned, and walked out of the bedroom, leaving Michael sitting in bed.

She had given him something to think about and he knew she was right-- it was up to him.

The summer passed. Soon it was September with the signs of autumn showing up everywhere. By this time Michael had prematurely convinced himself that he was doing well emotionally and mentally. Since Chris was included on all the business contracts that her father had, she had taken on her share of her father's business. Because she was living at home now, she flew three days of the week, giving her time to keep up with her college courses via e-mail. This left Michael to fly the plane the rest of the week, giving him more time to be with Cindy and their two younger daughters.

Cindy was back to being a mom, spending what spare time she had going to estate sales, looking for items for the "Practical Shop" in town. Grace and Melissa got to know each other very well, spending a lot of time in the attic sorting and sharing all the memories stored there. Jenny had returned to her home and family and gone back to counseling at her office in town, and Sherrie Henderson, her college friend and fellow counselor, packed her things and returned to her home up north.

On the surface, it looked like life had returned to normal for the Jacobson family. But we all know that appearances are usually deceiving. Another storm of a different kind was forming on the horizon, a storm that would place Melissa right in front of someone from her past that she needed to face.

The Orphan's Cry

"You will know that forgiveness has begun when you recall those who hurt you and feel the power to wish them well."

Lewis B. Smedes, Forgive & Forget:
Healing the Hurts We Don't Deserve

Melissa loved living at her old home again. She and Cindy had redecorated the bedroom she slept in as a teenager. Melissa loved her work at the cement and gravel company. She usually finished there at 3:30 p.m. After that she went to her part-time job at city hall, where she worked in the records department until 6:00 p.m.

Then one day, something out of the ordinary began to happen. Melissa didn't notice it at first, but someone was following her. She would catch glimpses of a woman watching her whenever she would leave the cement company and go to her part-time job. Sometimes she would see this same woman following her when she went out for lunch. It didn't concern her until the same woman started appearing more often. One time Melissa caught a glimpse of her looking in the window of the deli, where she was eating lunch.

What she saw was an attractive, slender woman, blond-haired with a little gray around the edges, and a sad expression on her face. A month of this human cat-and-mouse game made Melissa edgy. She thought of contacting the police, but decided to talk to Grace one late September evening while they were labeling some boxes in the attic.

Grace was looking at some old faded photographs when Melissa brought up the subject, telling her about the mysterious woman who seemed to be stalking her.

"Has she made any contact with you?" Grace asked. "Has she spoken to you or introduced herself? Who do you think she is?" Melissa looked at her, shrugging her shoulders. "She hasn't spoken to me yet because she always keeps her distance, and no, I don't know who she is."

Grace snapped her fingers on her right hand. "I got it. Get one of those cheap throwaway cameras and get some pictures of her. Bring the pictures back and I'll see if I can recognize her."

Melissa got up off the floor and walked down the stairs, leaving Grace by herself. The next day Melissa bought a disposable camera and waited. Sure enough, around lunch time the mysterious woman appeared. She stopped, looking right in the deli window at Melissa. Melissa quickly pulled the camera from her purse, taking several pictures of her.

The woman smiled at her at first. But when she saw the camera she frowned, covered her face with her coat, and ran. Later that day Melissa got the pictures developed. When she got home that evening she found Grace. Saying nothing, she pulled the pictures from her purse and handed them to her.

Grace studied the pictures. Then she got a strange look on her face. "That's our old high school math teacher Evelyn Thompson. I know, because Michael had a big crush on her. Is this the mystery lady that's been following you?"

Suddenly Melissa's face turned white, her eyes widening. She sat down with a thud on a nearby couch.

"Melissa, what's the matter?" Then Grace gasped and sat down with the same thud right next to Melissa, realizing who the woman was. They sat there for a short while, then turned, facing each other.

Melissa spoke first. "Evelyn is my birth mother, Grace." Then her face reddened. "Why is that woman following me after all these years? She gave me up like I was nothing to her--a throwaway child!" Melissa turned away from Grace and sat in silence for a moment with tears starting to form in her eyes. Then she looked back at her sister. "I spent six years of my life being passed from one foster home to another. Nobody wanted me until your mother and aunt adopted me. Now I finally find a family that I can call my own and she shows up. I hate her, Grace!"

Grace pulled her into her arms and held her. A short while later, Grace spoke. "I know one thing. I'm glad she didn't abort you. I don't know what I would've done if I'd found out that you were my sister and never had the chance to get to know you and love you the way I do now."

Melissa sighed, smiled, and hugged her back. "Thank-you, I love you too."

At that same moment on the outskirts of town, in her snug little two- bedroom house, Evelyn Thompson was all alone with only her thoughts to keep her company. She knew that Melissa had seen her and had taken pictures of her. It wouldn't be long before she found out who she was. She threw the box of tissues she was holding across her living room. "Why," she thought, "did I have to get involved with Roger Jacobson?" She smiled slightly. "She does have her father's eyes. That's one thing that attracted me to her." She sighed. "I want to hold my daughter again, regardless of how old she is. It's been too many years, and I'm aching to hold her just once!" Evelyn walked over to the living room window and looked out. She thought, "I'm just going to have to face her and tell her the truth--how much of a coward I was; how I don't deserve to be her real mother." She turned and sat down on her couch with tears starting to form in her eyes again.

Back at the Jacobson home, Grace let go of Melissa and sighed. "Now that she knows you've recognized her, she'll probably want to get together with you. I know you don't want anything to do with her. But look at it from her side. She's probably regretted what she did to you, and still loves you otherwise she wouldn't watch you the way she has."

Melissa looked at her with her face starting to get red again. "Grace, she abandoned me! She practically left me on the doorstep of the adoption agency. Do you call that love? I call it not being responsible. I believe if you make children you should care for them, not aborting them like they were nothing but a cyst, or giving them away like they were an unwanted toy!"

Grace took Melissa by her shoulders. "Melissa, sometimes there are other reasons why a mother has to give up her child for adoption. But regardless of what Evelyn's reasons were, you still need to go and talk to her. Let her explain her side of the story. After she has, you can thank her for being honest with you, for telling you the truth. Then you can get up and walk out of her life."

Melissa sighed, taking Grace's hands off her shoulders. "You're right. As much as I don't want to, I should." She looked down at the floor for a minute, then back at Grace. "This is so strange. What if I end up wanting her back as my mom? I mean, there's this craving inside of me to want to get to know her and be loved by her. Does that sound crazy to you?"

"No, that sounds the way it should be between a mother and her daughter. Don't you think you should forgive her and be a friend to her?"

Grace smiled, looking at the clock on the family room wall. "Let's go make some dinner for that hungry family of ours."

Up in the air, Michael and Chris had just flown in from the mainland with some new parts for their plane. It was getting dark, and Michael was just starting to make his circle to land on their runway when both engines suddenly stopped! Lights flashed and warning devices began to sound as the plane started to lose altitude.

Chris, who was half asleep, sat straight up. "Oh my God! Both engines just quit!"

Michael looked over at his daughter. "Try to keep calm, Chris; things like this happen. Try looking out your side window for someplace to land."

"Okay, I'll keep cool. I'll keep cool. Dad! There's a landing strip to the right of us!"

With nothing but the sound of air whistling around the plane's cabin, Michael banked the plane to the right. "You're right, Chris. Let's drop in on these nice people and thank them for the use of their runway." Michael turned the plane around, lining it up with the runway below them. Ignoring all the lights that were flashing, Michael lowered the landing gear. As soon as the wheels touched down, Michael began to slow the plane down, using the aircraft's brakes. He finally brought it to a stop in the backyard of the home that sat about two hundred yards off the runway.

Turning off the airplane's switches, Michael exhaled. "I knew this place looked familiar."

Chris wiped the sweat off her forehead. "It sure does. I wonder if they're home." She looked over at her dad, giving him a big hug. "Dad, you were terrific!"

Michael sighed and looked at her. "If you were all alone up there and this happened to you, do you think you could've handled it?"

She smiled back. "If I had to, I could. But I'm sure glad you were with me when it did."

Suddenly the back door of the house opened and

a couple ran up to Michael and Chris's plane. Michael opened the plane's cabin door. "I hope we didn't surprise you too much by dropping in unannounced."

Dan looked up at him and smiled. "Are you kidding? We didn't hear you land. Jenny just happened to look out our kitchen window and yelled that there was a plane in our backyard. I thought that was strange because ours is in the hangar. Well, come in, you two. We'll make a fresh pot of coffee and you can explain why you snuck up on us like you did."

Inside the kitchen, all four of them had just sat down at the kitchen table with their coffee. Michael looked straight at Dan. "Are you two doing anything tomorrow? I need help with my plane."

Dan looked at Jenny and back at Michael. "Well, we thought we'd drop our daughters off at your house and do a little shopping down in Manchester just south of us. What about your plane?"

Michael continued, "Both my engines just died on me about a thousand feet up while I was making my usual circle to land on our runway. I knew I had to land somewhere fast and here we are."

Dan turned, looking at Jenny who kissed him on his forehead. "Go for it, big boy."

He grinned, turning to look at Michael. "Oh man, it could be anything. With a plane as old as yours, it could be wiring, a circuit board could have fried, a broken fuel line. Who knows until we get into it? I'm just glad you landed safely."

"Is there any way we can get my plane into your hangar so we can work on it?"

Dan smiled. "Sure is. I just made a special tow

bar for the front of my old pickup truck, and I'm sure it will fit your plane."

Dan, Michael, and Chris walked out of the kitchen door and over to the hangar. Dan lifted the door, got into his old pickup and started it up. Dan drove it over to the front of Michael's plane, got out, and looked at Michael. "Lower the tow bar and hold the forked part just above your front wheel, then guide it on and lock it in place."

Once the tow bar was in place, Dan had Chris walk along one wingtip and Michael on the other. Dan maneuvered the plane with his truck until he lined it up with the open hangar door. Once the plane was backed into the hangar alongside Dan's plane, Michael unhooked the tow bar, raising and fastening it to the front of Dan's truck.

Dan turned off the motor to his truck and got out. "Okay, let's take off the access panels to the wings and check the wiring harnesses. Then we'll start running continuity tests to see if we can find any breaks. We'll pull the fuel lines, checking them along with the fuel bladders. I think the engines are okay, but we'll check them too." Then he looked at Michael. "We'd better go into town tomorrow and rent that Cessna Frank Clayton has at the airport. You're going to need a ride until we can get yours going, right?"

Michael smiled. "Yes we are, but right now let's help Chris get her hands dirty. That should finish off the rest of those pretty finger nails of hers!" Chris made a face at her dad, rolling up the sleeves to the blouse she was wearing. All of them worked on the plane until midnight.

Michael looked at his watch. "I think I've had it for tonight. Chris and I will be back tomorrow and ride into town with you to pick up that Cessna. Does 9:00 a.m. sound okay to you?"

Dan was on his back in the plane with his head stuck up under the instrument panel. "That's fine. Besides, I think I've found part of your problem." Shortly after midnight, Cindy sat in Dan and Jenny's driveway, sounding the horn on the station wagon. Michael and Chris were washing the last of the degreasing solution off their arms in the kitchen, then said their good-byes and left the house.

As Michael got into the station wagon, he leaned over and kissed Cindy. "Thanks for coming over this late and picking us up, sweetheart." Cindy looked at him for a moment, playfully tapping his forehead with her finger. "See, it does pay to be responsible when you're up there, doesn't it?"

Michael spoke sharply. "What do you mean by that?"

Cindy just shot him a "gotcha" look and started the motor.

On the way home Chris, who had been thinking about what her mom had just said to her dad, suddenly made a face. "Excuse me, Mom, but Dad was terrific up there! He had his radio on, he landed safely, and you didn't have to shoot anything at him either!"

Suddenly Cindy's face turned redder than the top she was wearing. She'd forgotten that she'd told Chris about the radio incident months ago; now Chris was using her own words against her. She sighed. "You're right, Chris. I'm sorry. I should be thankful you two landed safely."

The next morning Michael and Chris went into town with Dan to look at the Cessna at the airport. Melissa left to go to work at her job in town, while Grace helped Cindy clean up after breakfast. After Abby had climbed on her bus to go to school, Grace took Sarah to the living room and played with her. Cindy retreated to her craft room just off the kitchen and began to work on some centerpieces for the "Practical Shop." She was trying to make sense of a pile of artificial fall leaves and where they went on the centerpiece she was working on. She glanced at a photo of Michael and her taken when they were still in college, pinned to her craft idea board.

"Michael and I were so young then," she thought to herself. "That picture was taken after I kissed him at the football game. Maybe I shouldn't have, but I wanted to get to know him so much. I had seen him on campus several times, hoping he would notice me, but he never did. I don't know what it was that made me kiss him. Part of me felt like a fool and the other part of me said go for it. I'm glad I did, because he was worth it.

"Three wonderful daughters later, this mess with his abuse shows up and causes havoc with our family. I honestly don't know where it's going, but I hope it ends soon. Now we have Grace and a new half sister added to the family. That's good, because I love them both and they're a real help with the girls and the house. I could say that life has been good to us, regardless of all the trials in our lives… but…trials are good. Good because they build character and make us resilient. I love my family and it would have been terrific if my mom and dad could've known them. But they died just like Jenny's did in a car accident. I guess that's why I'm so glad Michael came along when he did... but... wait a minute. Maybe I haven't allowed myself to grieve their loss. I should talk to Jenny about that."

Cindy was still standing at her craft table, mindlessly sifting the pile of leaves, when Michael walked in and leaned against the door frame that opened into the craft room from the kitchen. He stood there saying nothing until Cindy suddenly turned, walking right into him. She jumped back as he laughed. "Hi, nice of you to run into me. We should do this more often."

Cindy stood there motionless for a moment, then threw her arms around his neck, kissing him. "How long have you been standing there looking at me?" Michael looked around and back at her. "Oh, long enough to watch you sift through that silly pile of leaves at least seven or eight times."

"I guess I'm not getting anything done here. Let's make a pot of chili and bake some cornbread. I haven't had it for a while, and I know you love it." She took her arms from around his neck and walked into the kitchen.

Michael rubbed his stomach, grinning. "Yes, one pot for me and one pot for the rest of you." Cindy laughed, mentioning something about his eyes being bigger than his stomach.

Later when everyone had eaten way too much and had gone their separate ways, Melissa and Cindy were in the kitchen cleaning up. Suddenly Melissa looked up from the table she was wiping off and looked at Cindy. "What would you do if you were adopted and you found out your birth mother was trying to get together with you again?"

Cindy's thoughts had been on what she was going to make for breakfast the next day. She turned from the sink and faced her. "I'm sorry, could you please repeat what you just said?"

Melissa started over. "Evelyn Thompson, my birth mother, has been following me around for weeks. The other day I took some pictures of her staring at me through a window at the deli where I eat lunch. My question is, should I get together with her?"

"Let's go sit in the nook."

Melissa sat down in a chair opposite Cindy at the table. She folded her hands neatly in front of her, waiting for Cindy to respond. Cindy looked at her and sighed. "I think you ought to hear her side of the story. She probably hasn't forgiven herself for giving you away and is probably feeling guilty. She obviously wants to see you. Melissa, you aren't the only one that was abandoned. Evelyn was abandoned by your birth father, Roger. He obviously didn't want the responsibility of raising you, and he couldn't face his wife like a man and tell her that he had an affair. Right after he signed the adoption papers, he was killed in a hunting accident, leaving her all alone with a baby that she didn't want in the first place. What would you have done?"

Melissa frowned. "If I were her, I wouldn't have had an affair with that rat of a father I had."

Cindy shook her head. "With Roger the rat aside, what would you have done?"

Melissa sighed. "I would have gone through with the pregnancy and had the baby and been the mom I should have."

Cindy looked at her, smiling slightly. "I believe you probably would have. But the truth is, you're not Evelyn. If you think about it, she probably chose to give you up because of fear. Once she found out she was pregnant, she probably took a leave of absence from her teaching job just to have you. A pregnancy isn't something you can hide. She may have had to move out of town temporarily, staying with a relative or a friend until she had you. Melissa, do you realize what gossip and scandal would have done to her, had the town found out? She could have lost her job and had her reputation ruined."

All this time, Melissa sat listening to Cindy with her hands folded and her head down. After a while, she slowly raised her head looking at Cindy. "So, do you think I'm selfish? Do you feel that I should just go, throw myself into her arms, and tell her all is forgiven?"

Cindy pondered her answer. "Let's look at this differently. Instead of you going to visit her and spilling out all the anger and hurt you have inside, why don't you put your feelings aside, asking her what her life was like growing up as a girl? Find out what her likes and dislikes are. Pick her brain; ask her questions, getting her to talk. I can guarantee she'll tell you everything you need to know. Then you can make your decision on how far your relationship should go with her. The idea is to help you understand your mother-- who she is and what she's gone through. Who knows? It may just defuse some of the anger and hurt you have inside. The ball's on your side of the court. Now you have to decide how you want to play it."

Cindy got up from the table, leaving Melissa alone by herself in the kitchen. Melissa slowly walked over to the phone that hung on the kitchen wall. She looked through the phone book that sat on a small table next to it, then picked up the receiver, punching in some numbers on it. Biting her lip nervously, she waited until a man answered on the other end.

"Dave? Hi, this is Melissa. I was wondering if I could have Monday off. I know it's really short notice, but I would like it off anyway." She waited for his response, then smiled. "Thanks, Dave. Oh don't worry; I finished those contracts on Friday. They're over on the filing cabinet in the out basket."

Monday morning Michael and Chris took off in the rented Cessna for the mainland. Abby had just gotten on her bus and Sarah was still asleep in her room. Cindy, Grace, and Melissa were sitting in the nook drinking their coffee when Melissa looked at her watch.

"Well, I've got to go. I'll see you later."

Cindy grabbed her arm as she got up to leave. "Are you going to meet with Evelyn?" Melissa smiled and nodded. Cindy was pleased. "I'm glad you're doing this. Remember it's not just for you; it's for her too."

"I know. Don't save any supper for me; I may not be back until late."

With that she walked over to the wooden rack

on the wall, took her purse, and left. Grace looked at Cindy. "How did you get her to do that?"

"Well, I got Melissa to get her mind off herself. Life is not just a 'me doing my own thing'; it's an 'us working together and loving each other through it thing.' Melissa knows all too well what she went through. Now she's going to learn what Evelyn had to go through."

It was ten thirty when Melissa drove her car into the parking lot of the deli where she ate her lunch every day. She turned off the engine and looked at the makeup on her face in her visor mirror before getting out. Once inside, she ordered an espresso and sat down at a table by the front window. Melissa sat there looking out the window for a moment, then glanced down, spotting a phone book that someone had left there. She opened it and started to look for Evelyn's home phone number. Melissa was about to call her on her cell phone when she looked up. There was Evelyn looking back at her through the deli window. Evelyn knew that Melissa had recognized her and took off, walking away as fast as she could. Melissa threw her cell phone in her purse, got up, and ran out of the deli. Evelyn had just turned the corner, about to hail a taxi, when Melissa grabbed hold of her arm.

Evelyn turned and faced her. Both women said nothing as they stood there looking at each other, then Melissa took a deep breath and let it out. "Please don't go. I need to talk with you."

Evelyn stood there in silence for a moment. Then she sighed. "I guess we could go to my house. I didn't drive today. We could share a taxi, unless you have a car."

Melissa offered the use of her car, asking Evelyn for directions. On the way there nothing was said between them. Melissa glanced over only twice at Evelyn, who kept looking out the side window of the car, nervously twisting and untwisting the straps on her purse with her hands.

Suddenly Evelyn pointed in the direction of her home. "Here it is. Just turn in the driveway and park next to the rose bush on the left."

Melissa drove into the driveway. Both women got out of the car and walked over to the front door of the house. It was a ranch style single level, with well-manicured flowers in front. Evelyn was fumbling with the contents of her purse, trying to find her house keys, when she spoke up.

"I'm sorry. I'm not normally like this. Please forgive me." Melissa looked at her. "It's okay. Just take your time."

But Melissa was not okay; she was in turmoil. She appeared calm on the outside, but she really wanted to yell at and hit Evelyn. Evelyn finally got the front door open, walking quickly to a coat rack where she hung up her coat. She turned, facing Melissa who stood just inside the doorway, trembling.

"Please come in, Melissa. Would you like some tea? I can make some for us."

Melissa mechanically nodded, walked in, and closed the door. She took off her coat, laying it down with her purse on a chair. Evelyn walked into her kitchen to make the tea, leaving Melissa in the living room alone. She looked at some pictures, carefully picking up some small curios from a shelf.

Melissa was looking at one of them when Evelyn walked in with a tray holding a teapot, two cups with saucers, and some cookies on a plate.

She looked at Melissa, trying to smile. "I hope you like earl gray tea. Would you like some cookies I made this morning?"

Melissa looked at her and put the curio she was looking at back on the shelf. "Yes, whatever you made is fine with me." Evelyn set the tray on the coffee table in front of the couch and sat down, looking at Melissa. Melissa sat down on the opposite end of the couch.

"Do you take cream with your tea?"

Melissa nodded, taking one of the cookies off the tray. She took a bite out of it, then laid it down on the coffee table. She looked straight at her mother. "Who told you that I ate my lunch at that deli?"

Evelyn looked at her and sighed. "I started following you almost a year ago, when I nearly bumped into you once on the street. You have your father's eyes and that's what got me wondering who you were. Then I saw you go into the courthouse one day. I went in shortly after you, asking the security guard who you were. After he told me, I wanted to get to know you, but I was afraid and followed you at a distance. I hope I didn't cause you any concern by doing that."

Melissa shook her head. "I wasn't concerned, and I only recently noticed you. Do you mind if I ask, what was life like for you growing up as a girl?"

Evelyn wasn't expecting her to ask that. She really anticipated that Melissa would start yelling at her, telling her how horrible she was and that she wasn't fit to be any kind of a mother, especially hers. What Melissa said caught her off guard. Evelyn sat there for a moment with her eyes closed. She opened them, looking at her daughter. "Life for me as a girl was a challenge sometimes, because my parents, who were teachers, were always trying to project their own expectations onto me.

"Although my parents loved me, I still felt like life for me went by too quickly. I was a young woman in college earning a teaching degree before I sat down one day, realizing that I'd been cheated out of much of life, and angry that I couldn't go back and do it all over again.

"I finally graduated from college with honors. I came back to Crandon and got a job teaching math at the high school. Everything was going fine for me. I had plenty of friends and went to lots of parties." Then Evelyn looked down, studying the tea cup she was holding. Finally she looked at Melissa with her eyes tearing up. "Then I met Roger. He used to come into the coffee shop where I ate sometimes, where the deli is now. I didn't pay too much attention to him at first because I had a boyfriend at the time, but one day that all changed.

"I was sitting at the counter one day and he sat down right next to me, ordering his coffee and a piece of pie. I turned and looked at him, he looked at me, and I was hooked. I didn't know he was married. He didn't have a ring on, and he was really good looking. We started dating after that. One night we had too much to drink. I don't remember that night because it was a blur. All I know was that I had a terrible headache the next day and my body ached all over. I didn't see Roger for at least a couple of weeks after that. Then at the end of the month I didn't have my period as usual. I started to get scared and went to my doctor. Six days later he gave me the news." Evelyn closed her eyes, sighing. "I was pregnant with you."

Tears were running down Melissa's cheeks. She wanted to yell at Evelyn, but she couldn't. She wanted get up and start smashing things, but her legs wouldn't cooperate, so she couldn't get off the couch. Instead, she sat there in quiet desperation.

Evelyn cleared her throat. "I didn't know what to do or who to turn to. I hated myself so much that I thought about killing myself. I had the chance to abort you, but decided against it. As I look at you now, I'm glad I didn't. Instead, I took a one-year leave of absence from my teaching job. I had to act quickly because I was starting to show. I knew my sister was very understanding, so I left town and stayed up north with her until I had you.

"One day I signed some papers along with your father. Then I ended up doing one of the hardest things I've ever done in my life: I gave you away. I know you may not believe me, but it was." She wiped her eyes and sighed. "After that, I was never the same. I went through life like it was an emotional nightmare. I didn't want to see Roger, especially after I found out that he was married with two kids. When he and his brother were killed in a hunting accident, I came home and cried my eyes out, more out of depression than remorse. I didn't eat for days. I drank just to bury my hurt.

"Then one day I realized that drinking was an excuse not to face you. So I started watching you at a distance. I was cautious at first, then I got bolder, looking right at you one day through the deli window. That's the day you took those pictures of me. So here we are, finally meeting. I wouldn't blame you if you yelled and screamed at me or hit me. I deserve it."

Evelyn looked at Melissa, moving a little closer to her on the couch. "I wouldn't blame you if you got up and walked out of here, never wanting to see me again. I guess if I were you, I'd do the same." Then she stopped talking and looked away from her daughter.

Five minutes passed. Melissa slowly exhaled, wiping her eyes with some tissues she had. "I wanted to call you every horrible name I could think of. Yes, I wanted to hit you, but I realize now that you've been hurting just as much as I have, maybe more." Suddenly Melissa couldn't hold her emotions inside any longer and began to shake. "Please hold me and tell me that you love me for who I am!"

Melissa threw herself into her mother's open arms and burst into tears. Evelyn wrapped her arms around her daughter, holding her close. Finally, mother and daughter had broken out of their own individual hurts and into each other's hearts. Melissa and Evelyn talked late into the night. Melissa left, promising her mother that they would get together soon. When Melissa got out of her car that night, she felt like gravity had no pull on her. She looked up at the starry sky and whispered, "Thank you, God, for putting my mom and I back together again." She walked over to the back door, unlocked it, and went in. Cindy had left the kitchen lights on for her but had fallen asleep, sitting in the nook with her head resting on her folded arms.

Melissa bent over, kissing her on her forehead. Cindy yawned, looked up, and smiled. "I can tell by the look on your face that you two made up, didn't you?"

"Yes we did, and you were right. I listened to her side of the story, not spilling out any of my hurt on her, no matter how tempted I was."

Cindy stretched, got up, and turned off the kitchen lights. Then both of them climbed the back stairs together.

October came, chilling the trees that bordered the meadow, painting their leaves with the brilliant colors of the season. The last flocks of birds were flying southward. Evening was settling in on the Jacobson home. Dinner was over and everyone had gone to their rooms to finish out the night.

Grace was in her bedroom, sitting in her rocking chair near one of the windows. She had a floor lamp turned on and was reading some of the letters she'd found in the attic with Jenny months earlier. Grace had just finished reading a packet of letters when a small, worn diary fell out if it. She picked it up and began to read. After going through a number of pages, she sat straight up in the rocking chair, shaking her head in disbelief. She got up and walked over to her purse that hung on a pegged rack near the bedroom door. She pulled out her cell phone and called Jenny.

"Hello, Jenny? I'm sorry I've called you this late, but I found an old diary written by Abigail Jacobson in a packet of old letters. She made an entry one day, describing something that happened to Jacob Jacobson, Michael's great-great grandfather. I think you'd better read it."

After Jenny agreed to read it the next day, Grace turned off her cell phone, putting it back in her purse. She continued to read the diary as she walked back to the rocking chair, sitting down in it. Shocked at what she was reading, she put the diary down only long enough to look out one of her bedroom windows across the moonlit meadow, toward the old mill that sat across the lake. Grace thought she saw lights moving around inside the old mill, but decided it was her imagination playing tricks on her. Who would be in that old wreck of a building at this time of night? She laid the diary down on her dresser, turned out the floor lamp, climbed into bed, and fell asleep.

The next morning after breakfast, Jenny called to say she was on her way over. Twenty minutes later she drove up and parked beside the carport. She got out of her SUV, walked over to the back door, and opened it.

"Is anyone home?" Grace was sitting in the nook. "Come on in, Jenny. Cindy's upstairs. She'll be down in a minute."

Jenny looked at her and smiled. "You know I want to get my hands on that old diary, but I promised Cindy that I'd take a walk with her first. I hope you don't mind."

Grace returned the smile, but quickly raised

her eyebrows. "When you read it, you'll see where the pattern of abuse starts in our family." Then she sighed. "Jenny, I'm getting closer to forgiving my father and uncle, but my heart's not there yet."

Jenny looked at her for a moment before answering. "That's okay, Grace. You'll know when it is."

Just then, Cindy came down the back stairs and into the kitchen. "Are you ready to take a walk with me? I looked outside this morning and the colors on the trees are gorgeous. I thought we could take some apples and granola bars with us."

Jenny smiled. "I canceled all my appointments; you got me for the whole day."

Cindy grabbed a backpack with the snacks in it off the kitchen counter as both the women walked out the back door, closing it behind them. They had walked down the old logging road just a short distance when they found the old log that Grace had mentioned earlier. Jenny spread a blanket out on it and both of them sat down. Cindy put the backpack down and opened it. Jenny reached in, pulling out an apple. She took a bite out of it and sighed. "A beautiful day, great fall colors, a good friend, and a tasty apple. I couldn't ask for anything better."

Cindy grimaced. "Now I have to ruin it by asking you to listen to what I have to say."

Jenny squeezed Cindy's arm, smiling. "You aren't ruining it. Besides, what you have to say means a lot to me."

Cindy cleared her throat before beginning her story. "My parents and sister and I lived in a small town in southwest Michigan. Our home was a hundred-year-old farm house that had been a doctor's office at one time. My dad worked at the local post office as a mail carrier and my mom took in sewing. I used to love the autumn and fall seasons. School was okay, but I liked going to the county fair better. I loved it when Christmas came around. My mom loved it too.

"Time passed and too many Christmases later, my sister and I found ourselves all grown up. I was eighteen and my sister was seventeen when our parents were killed in a car accident. I'll never forget that day. It was snowing outside, and my sister and I had just gotten home from school. We were getting ready to bake some Christmas cookies when the doorbell rang. I went to the front door covered with flour. I opened it and there stood a policeman and a policewoman. I let them in and they took off their hats and coats, laying them on my dad's organ bench."

Tears formed in Cindy's eyes as she continued. "I knew something was wrong just by looking at their faces. The policeman said that our parents' car had been hit by a coiled roll of steel coming off a semitruck flatbed trailer. Then the policewoman said that the truck driver had been killed when his truck slid and slammed into a bridge support. She said our parents were killed when the roll of steel broke loose and rolled over their car, crushing them both. My sister started crying and I went into shock. That was the worst Christmas I have ever had.

"Life for me flew by in a blur after that. I lived

from day to day, not feeling much at all. I just functioned. Somehow, a few years later, I found myself in college, taking classes, faking my way through life. Then one day at a football game, I saw this cute guy sitting next to an attractive red-headed girl named Jenny. I assumed she was his girlfriend and decided to have a little fun. So I got up, turned around, and kissed him. The rest you know.

"Over the years, I fashioned my perfect little world around Michael, the girls, you and Dan. I used that perfect world as an excuse to bury the grief over the loss of my parents deep inside me. I know I'll have to deal with it sooner or later, or the truth will eat away at all the excuses I've made for not facing it. I guess that's why you're sitting on this log with me right now. I need to grieve but I don't know how. I want to forgive that truck driver, but I can't. I want to forgive my parents for leaving me too soon, but I can't do that either. My heart's locked up, and I need help to unlock it.

"Then there's all this mess with Michael's family. I know it may sound silly, but is there any way God and you can work something out? You're my best friend, Jenny. I really need your help."

Jenny sat there looking at Cindy for a while, absorbing what she'd just heard. "No, it doesn't sound silly. I do know that God works on his own. He doesn't need to consult me or you on what he does or how he does it. The only thing we need to do is work with him when he tells us to do something." Then she smiled. "As far as I'm concerned, I'll do my best. You're absolutely right; you do need to grieve, and you need to forgive that truck driver and your parents. Not for their sakes, but for yours."

Cindy looked down at a tall wildflower that was turning brown, then at Jenny. "You're right. Do you have any suggestions?"

"I suggest that you get a hold of your sister, regardless of how long it's been since you've seen her. I have a gut feeling that you two should get together and work this out. Once you get in contact with her, all three of us could get together and talk. For now, can we get back? I promised Grace that I'd go over an old diary that she found last night."

Cindy and Jenny got up, folded the blanket they were sitting on, grabbed the backpack, and started walking back to the house. Back in the kitchen, Grace was pacing back and forth across the kitchen floor when Jenny and Cindy walked through the back door. Grace exhaled. "It's about time you two showed up. I was beginning to think you'd walked to Crandon and back."

Jenny complimented Grace. "We took your advice on that log. You're right; it's a great place to sit and talk. So where's that diary you're so anxious for me to look at?"

Grace pulled the diary out of her apron pocket and handed it to Jenny. Jenny took it, walked over to the kitchen nook, sat down, and started to read. After she had read about halfway through it, she shook her head, looking at Grace sitting across from her. "You're right. The pattern of abuse did start with one of Michael's ancestors. From what Abigail put in her diary, it was with a drunken Native American who just happened to be a pedophile. It's a tragedy it had to happen to her husband Jacob, Michael's great-great grandfather. Now I know where it started and where it has to end. Both of you still need to forgive your dad and uncle for what they did."

Jenny looked at Grace and continued. "The healing process, however long it takes, can't start until both of you choose to forgive. God gave you the freedom and the ability to make those choices, but he won't make them for you. You're responsible for your choices, just like everyone else. When you face him at the end of your life and you haven't forgiven the people that have hurt you, he'll hold you accountable. I'm not saying all this because I want to scare you or to make God into some sort of tyrant. I'm saying this because I love both you and your brother. I don't want to see you or your family held in this emotional and mental prison by giving evil the legal right to keep you there."

Jenny stood up, stretching. "I've got to get home. Cindy, please remember what I said about your sister and get back to me when all of us can meet." Jenny got up from the nook, walked over to the back door, and left.

Cindy nodded. "Jenny's right, Grace. It seems that all of us are faced with the decision to forgive. What do you think?"

Grace looked at Cindy and sighed. "Yes, it seems we are. Well, I know what I have to do. With my brother, it may take something else to help him realize what he needs to do."

It was the second week in October on a Friday night. Michael was burning leaves in the fire pit that he and the family had raked and bagged up. Everyone was sitting around the fire on folding chairs with long sticks, toasting marshmallows. Michael had just filled the fire bucket with water and sat down next to Grace when one of the marshmallows on Grace's stick fell off into the fire. Grace looked at the marshmallow burning, glanced at the water bucket, and began to laugh.

Michael looked at his sister with a grin. "If it's so funny, why don't you tell me all about it?"

"Do you remember our old sheepdog Rex?"

"Sure I do. What about him?"

"One night you and I and Mother and Father were toasting marshmallows over a fire not too far from this spot. Rex, as usual, was sleeping much too close to the fire when one of the marshmallows fell off my stick into the fire just like this one. It landed right by Rex's nose and exploded. What a hot, gooey mess."

Michael laughed as he finished the story. "It sure was. Rex howled, jumped up, and ran around, knocking us off our chairs, finally sticking his head into the water bucket a little too hard. His head got stuck in it and he ran around backwards, shaking the bucket and throwing water all over everyone. You and I had to pick bits of sticky marshmallow out of the fur around his nose with him kicking and squirming. That was a lot of fun!"

Grace looked away from Michael at the fire in front of them and smiled. "Wouldn't it be wonderful to go back and share the happy times we had? I mean, before you were abused, it seemed like we were always laughing." Then she leaned over sideways, resting her head against one of his shoulders.

Michael put his arm around his sister. He stared into the fire for a while. "You know, I don't think it would matter to me, Grace. If you added all the happiness and all the sadness up, they cancel each other out, resulting in...nothing."

Grace turned her head and looked up at him. "I wouldn't say that. We still have each other." Michael looked down at her and smiled, but said nothing. Grace turned her head back toward the fire again.

"Michael, our lives are so fragile. One day we're here and the next day we're gone, like a flame that dances its way across time until one day it just goes out." She looked back up at Michael, turning his face towards hers with one of her hands. "I'm tired of living trapped inside my own emotions. I'm giving up my right to hold our father and uncle responsible for what they did to us. I'm choosing to forgive them, whether they deserve it or not. Michael, please let God help you out of the prison you're in. I'd love to see you freed of all this mess. But it's up to you. You're the one that has to let go and forgive."

She slowly got up from her chair. She walked over, saying something to Cindy. Cindy looked over at Michael who was staring into the fire. "Michael, the wind is starting to pick up and it looks like rain. Why don't you put the fire out and come in the house?"

Michael was still trying to sort out what Grace had just told him. Saying nothing, he got up and picked up the water bucket, slowly pouring water over the fire. Sure enough, the wind was beginning to pick up as Michael walked with the others back to the house.

The Place Of Surrender

"When we forgive evil we do not excuse it, we do not tolerate it, we do not smother it. We look the evil full in the face, call it what it is, let its horror shock and stun and enrage us, and only then do we forgive it."

Lewis B. Smedes - Forgive & Forget:
Healing the Hurts We Don't Deserve

The end of October had come with the busy little town of Crandon celebrating its annual October harvest festival. At the Jacobson home Chris finished taking her final exams via e-mail, passing with flying colors. Melissa was still working in town and visited her mother often. Cindy was designing craft items for the "Practical Shop" in town, still playing the role of wife, mother, and business owner. Michael's plane was repaired, so he was back to flying along with Chris. Grace had taken on the role of housekeeper, babysitter, and part-time cook, and like her mother before her, had started painting.

One cold, crisp October morning a blue Ford pickup truck pulled up next to the old hangar where Michael was working on his plane. Michael heard someone knocking on the door, so he put down his wrench, wiping his hands on a rag nearby. He opened the entrance door to the hangar, surprised to see their pastor standing there. "Jim! I thought you kept banker's hours, spending most of your time at church."

Jim Thatcher smiled. "I stopped by the deli this morning and picked up some of those Bavarian cream-filled rolls you're drooling over all the time. I thought we could eat them along with that sludge over there you call coffee."

Michael grinned. "At least you can drink it. If you don't want to drink it, you can waterproof your basement walls with it."

Both men laughed. Then Jim's smile softened. "Michael, have you got some time to take a walk with me down the old logging road?"

Michael pointed to one of the rolls. "You wouldn't make me take a walk without the nourishment that these great rolls provide, would you?"

Jim laughed. "Of course I wouldn't deny you your sugar fix. Just do me a favor and don't go into sugar shock while we're out there, because I am not going to carry you back."

Michael tried to laugh but couldn't. He had a roll stuck halfway into his mouth. Later in the morning, after two and a half rolls and two cups of coffee flavored sludge, Michael and Jim took off walking down the old road, finally stopping at the old log that he and his sister used to sit on.

Jim looked at Michael. "This seems like a good place to sit and talk."

Michael sat down on the log opposite Jim. Jim

took a deep breath and let it out. "You and Cindy sure have a beautiful piece of God's country out here."

Michael looked around, nodding. "I agree with you; it's a great piece of real estate."

Jim's face turned serious. Michael studied it for a moment. "Are you feeling okay?"

"I was just about to ask you the same thing. What was going on with you the day I put my arm around you-- the day we worked on our planes in your hangar?"

Michael looked down at the ground for a moment, then he looked up at Jim. "I had a flashback of my dad and uncle with liquor bottles in their hands. They seemed so real it scared me. I'm just glad you were there."

Jim looked at him and frowned. "That may be part of it, but that's not the real reason, is it?"

Michael arched his eyebrows. "Cindy's been talking to Nancy, hasn't she?"

Jim sighed. "I'm your friend. I have been for the last fifteen years. Friends share things with each other and trust each other. I wouldn't betray the trust we have for anything in the world. Nancy wouldn't betray it either. She's a good wife and I love her. She cried off and on for days after Cindy told her about what had happened to you as a child, and she prays for you constantly."

Jim paused for a moment. "When are you going to forgive your father and uncle?"

Michael stared at him with a bitter look on his face. "I don't know! Every time I get close to forgiving them, I want them to die all over again."

"You really don't mean that, do you?"

Michael sighed. "No, but when I meet the guy in that hunting party that did kill them, I'm going to congratulate him on being a good shot, and thank him for doing the job for me."

Jim closed his eyes and shook his head. After a short pause, he opened them and looked at Michael. "When my older brother was killed in Vietnam, I couldn't forgive the enemy for what they did to him. I know it was an act of war, but I still hated the Vietcong. I made up my mind that from there on I was going to make the lives of every Asian person I knew miserable, and I did. When I was in high school I called them filthy names, I tore up their books and threw rocks at them. When they threatened to tell the principal on me, I threatened to beat them up. I had practically every Asian kid in that school so afraid of me that they turned and went the other way when they saw me coming, all except this one very attractive Asian girl. One day she walked right up to me and got in my face. She challenged me to hit her in front of everyone in the hall. Just then some of the kids I knew closed in around us, watching to see if I would take her up on it. I glared right back at her and raised my fist to hit her in her face, but I just couldn't do it.

"I couldn't make my arm move. I ended up calling her a dirty name and storming off, leaving her and the others standing in the hallway. A week later, this same girl came walking up to where the bus picked us up. She looked at me, saying, 'Come with me, please.' I didn't want to follow her, but I did.

"She found a bench in the schoolyard under a big maple tree and sat down. She sat there looking up at me, motioning for me to sit down. After I sat down, she looked me in the eyes.

"I heard your brother was killed in Vietnam.'

"I hissed back at her, "Yes, and you stinking gooks are the ones that did it!' Disregarding the slam I'd just made, she kept staring at me.

"I am so sorry for you that you lost your brother in my home country.'

"It was like someone had punched me in the stomach. 'You mean you're Vietnamese?" I got up to run, but she grabbed onto my arm, pulling me back down on the bench. She looked at me again, only this time she had tears running down her cheeks.

"My whole family died there.' She wiped the tears from her eyes with the sleeve of her coat. I sat there for a moment looking at her. For once I thought of someone else's pain instead of mine. Then I did something I never thought I would do. I swallowed my hate and pride and asked her what her name was.

"She spoke softly. 'My name is Chin Li, and what is yours?'

"I told her my name. Then I asked her how her family died.

"She sighed. 'There was a lot of fighting going on between American soldiers and the Vietcong. The Vietcong hide in village and use villagers like...' She held her notebook up in front of her.

"Like shields?'

"She nodded, looking down at the ground. 'Yes,

like shields. Anyway, American soldiers not know if they shoot the enemy or villagers. Everywhere people are running around yelling and screaming when all of a sudden an American soldier grabs me and pulls me out of the way. I see my family all running away. Then I see them all get shot. They all die!'

"She paused for a moment, deep in thought. Then she looked at me again.

"American soldier take me to helicopter and put me in. He gets in and then he is shot too. He falls in my lap and I hold him. Back at the American soldier's camp, I am taken to nurse's tent and she takes care of me. Later I am adopted by this nurse and I come here to America and go to school here. Then I see you hurt other Asian people and I ask them why you do that. The other students tell me that your brother was killed in Vietnam and you mad at Asian people because of it.'

"Then she gently took my face in her hands. 'That soldier who put me on helicopter, his name was Jack.'

"I knew in my heart it was my brother. Suddenly an emotional dam burst in me. I grabbed hold of her and held her in my arms. A lot of tears and pain spilled out of us in the short time we held each other on that bench. She let go of her grief for the loss of her family and I for the loss of my brother. I gave up my right to judge other people that day. Just because they looked different or spoke different or came from another country didn't give me the right to judge them based on my own hurt. I couldn't bring my brother back to life no matter how much I loved him or missed him. I will always cherish my memories of him. I will also cherish the memory of that day on that bench. It was there I learned to love people for what they were…a gift from God. Later I apologized to every Asian kid in the high school that I had hurt in one way or another. Chin Li and I became the best of friends. Her mother, a retired army nurse, became good friends with my family. One day she told us about the time she was in the MASH unit the day my brother died."

"Chin Li was a young teenager then, but now she's a grown woman. She married one of my high school buddies. They have two beautiful children, and they get together with Nancy and me all the time. Michael, I learned to forgive my brother's enemies, who became my enemies, through the pain of Chin Li's loss. I gave up my right to hold unforgiveness against them. I believe God is not only going to show you how to forgive your dad and uncle, but he's also going to show you his compassion, becoming the father that you had once, but lost."

Michael sat there in silence, then sighed. "Right, and why would God want to be a father to me? Besides, how can you see into my future?"

Jim shrugged his shoulders and smiled. "Well, I can't, but God can. Let's go back and share the rest of those rolls with your family, and please let's make some real coffee instead of that degreasing solution you keep in your hangar."

October passed with the remaining leaves depositing themselves around every nook and cranny of the house. By the first week of November, Michael had finished winterizing his plane. He was wiping his hands with a rag when Abby opened the entrance door to the hangar and yelled, "Dad, Mom told me to tell you that dinner's ready!" Then she ran back to the house.

He put the rag on his workbench and walked out of the hangar, turning off the hangar lights. As he shut the door to the hangar he looked up at the sky, noticing the heavy, gray snow clouds starting to cover the moon. Inside the kitchen it was warm and smelled of good things cooking. Michael walked in and hung his coat on its wooden peg next to the door. He washed his hands at the sink, then turned around, taking a deep breath of all the wonderful aromas before sitting down at the table.

Cindy was bending over the oven, pulling out a tray of cookies. Grace was stirring a pot of chili on the stove, and Melissa was setting the table. Chris had just come down the back stairs with Abby and Sarah and was getting them seated. Michael sat there quietly with a big smile on his face enjoying everything when, one by one, the women looked over at him and smiled. Cindy set the cookie tray down on the stove top, walked over, put her arms around his neck, and kissed him. "See, this proves how much we love you. You can enter a room quietly and we still know you're there."

Michael smiled. "I thank God that he gave us to each other, because I love all of you too."

Cindy looked at him and realized without a doubt that God had put them both together.

Time passed and it was two days after Thanksgiving. Cindy had just put the finishing touches on a Christmas wreath she had made. She took the wreath into the family room, hanging it on the chimney just above the mantelpiece. She looked at the pictures of Michael's parents and grandparents that she and Chris had found in the attic earlier that week. She touched each picture softly with her fingers as she rearranged them on the mantel.

Just then the phone on the kitchen wall rang. She walked out of the family room and into the kitchen, picking it up.

"Hello? Oh hi, Jenny. Yes, I just finished it about the same time I finished ours. Yes, I know how picky Mrs. Richardson is about her Christmas decorations. No, Michael is not back yet. He is probably taking his time because of the weather and all the Christmas mail and packages he has to deal with. Did we get the new all-wheel drive SUV? Yes, and I agree with Michael-- it was a smart decision. Now if the weather gets too bad he can use it instead of the plane. No, I don't think he will have too much problem with the ferry, because the coast guard keeps the ice broken up around the docks on the mainland and the docks on Water Street."

Cindy looked out the kitchen window as she heard a small aircraft overhead. "I think I hear him coming in now, Jenny. Do you want to meet this coming Monday morning at the bistro? Okay, yes, I'll bring Mrs. Richardson's wreath, uh-huh, bye."

Cindy hung up the phone, walked over to the sink, and washed her hands. Then she remembered that she left the hot glue gun on in the craft room. Cindy walked into the craft room, turning off the glue gun and the lights, then walked back into the kitchen to finish making dinner. Cindy walked over to the stove, turning on a burner to heat the water in the kettle. Just then, Michael opened the back door and walked in, stamping the snow off his boots on the doormat. He looked at Cindy as she stood at the stove, tasting her homemade stew with a wooden spoon.

"Whew! It may be cold and windy out there, but in here it's warm and it smells delicious!"

Cindy grinned, putting her warm arms around his cold neck, giving him a kiss. "There, does that warm you up?"

Michael squinted at her. "If you say so, but you taste like stew and that's making me hungry."

Cindy laughed. "Oh, go wash up, you big brat! Dinner will be ready soon. Would you please tell Melissa and Grace to come down and help me and tell Abby and Sarah they need to wash up too?" Michael was going up the back stairs when Cindy yelled at him. "I forgot to tell you that I am going to meet Jenny at the bistro Monday morning. If you have anything you want me to get in town, you'll have to let me know!"

Cindy was about to ladle the stew into some bowls when the phone rang. "Now who could that be?"

Cindy put the ladle back into the stew pot and answered the phone. As Cindy listened to the caller speaking, she looked out the kitchen window at the snow falling. She was hanging up the phone when Chris came down the back stairs.

Chris stopped and looked at her mother. "Mom,

what's wrong? You look worried."

Cindy looked and her and sighed. "Dr. Brogan just called."

"Is that something to be worried about?

"He wants your father to fly some blood plasma that the hospital there needs until they can get a shipment of their own."

Cindy turned away from her and looked out the kitchen window again.

"Mom, if it's going to save a life, it's important."

"You're right. It's just all that snow coming down that bothers me."

"Relax, Mom, Dad has flown in worse weather."

Later at the dinner table Cindy told Michael about the phone call, mentioning that Dr. Brogan would meet him at the airport.

Michael looked at Cindy. Then he got up from the table, walking over to the kitchen window and looking out. "The moon's trying to come out from behind the clouds. I guess I'd better get started." Michael walked over to the phone on the kitchen wall and called Dr. Brogan. After confirming that he was on his way, Michael hung up the phone, turning to Cindy who had just walked up to him. "Sweetheart, would you please…" Before he could finish what he was saying, she held up his freshly packed lunch bucket.

Chris cleared her throat. "Could you use a good copilot to keep you company?"

He walked over to the kitchen table where his oldest daughter was sitting and kissed her on her forehead. "There's nothing I'd rather do than have you up there with me…but not tonight."

Michael was walking toward the back door when he turned and looked at Cindy. "I should be back in a couple of hours or so, depending on weather conditions. If I'm not back in three hours, call Dan. I'll follow my usual flight plan to the mainland and back, except this time I'll stop at the airport in town and pick up the plasma from Dr. Brogan. Please say a prayer for me."

Michael kissed Cindy, putting on his leather flight jacket with the wool insert. Picking up his lunch bucket, he opened the back door. An icy blast of snow and wind greeted him. Michael closed the door behind him, wading through the snow to the hangar, opened the door, and went in. He walked over to his plane and opened a cabin door, putting his lunch bucket next to the pilot's seat. He opened the larger hangar door, climbed into the plane, and started its engines. He drove it outside the hangar closing the main door with the remote control he had.

Fortunately for Michael, the falling snow had started to let up, long allowing him to see the runway lit up by the moon. He eased the throttles forward and taxied the plane out onto the runway, glancing at his instrument panel to see if he had turned on the plane's wing deicers. He smiled, knowing that Matt Freeman always kept the runway and the entrance to his hangar cleared of snow and ice. Matt checked the runway almost every day to see if it needed plowing and salting. Matt had bought a used county dump truck with a snow plow on the front of it. He was proud of the work he did on Michael's runway, and Michael was happy to pay Matt to do it.

Back in the house, Cindy and Chris listened as the wind slowly drowned out the sound of the plane's engines.

Cindy looked at Chris. "Let's get those younger sisters of yours to bed. I still have to finish cleaning up in here, then I'm going to wait up for your dad."

Chris helped her mother clean up the kitchen. When all the dishes were washed and put away, the women climbed the back stairs, shutting off the kitchen lights on the way up.

In the meantime, Michael had just spotted Crandon's airport lights and started his landing approach. He touched down on one of the airport's runways, already cleared of snow and ice. Michael slowed the plane down as a set of automobile headlights flashed on and off. Assuming it was Dr. Brogan, Michael slowly taxied his plane over to where the car was parked and turned off his engines. Then he unbuckled his seat belts, got out, and walked over to the car. Dr. Brogan got out, smiling at Michael.

"I'm so glad you could do this for me."

Michael grinned. "Hey, I'm glad I could. Is this the plasma?"

The doctor nodded. "There should be enough here for them until their own shipment arrives tomorrow. You'd better get going. The hospital's waiting for this. Once you're in the air, I'll call them and let them know you're on your way. Thanks again, my friend, and safe flying."

Michael gave Dr. Brogan a thumbs-up as he carried the case of plasma back to his plane. Michael strapped it into the seat next to his with the seat's safety belts. Then he fastened his own safety belts and closed the door to the plane's cabin. He glanced at his fuel gauge as he was releasing the plane's brakes. The strong headwind that he had been fighting all the way to the airport caused him to use too much of it. He'd have to get the plane's tanks filled once he got to the mainland.

Michael swung his plane around and headed back down the runway. Since there was no one in the airport's tower and no other planes taking off or landing, he got his plane into the air quickly. As Michael approached the mainland, he spotted Ellington Airport's beacon light. He called the tower, getting permission to land on runway number five. He also informed the air traffic controller that he had a case of plasma for the hospital.

Michael spoke into his mike again. "Could you have your fuel truck meet up with me? I need my tanks filled."

Michael landed his plane and taxied over to hangar six, stopped, and turned off the engines. Michael waited until he saw an ambulance pull up. He got out, handing the case of plasma to the driver. The driver thanked Michael and drove away just as the fuel truck pulled up. The driver got out, unrolled his fuel line, got a stepladder off his truck, and set it near one of the plane's wings. Then he climbed the ladder, taking off the cap to the fuel tank.

As he was filling the plane with fuel, he yelled at Michael walking toward him. "Is it cold enough for you?"

Michael grinned. "That reminds me of a joke I heard recently."

The driver smiled back. "Let's hear it."

Michael cleared his throat. "Well, there were these two old codgers standing in the snow one day, watching the air in their lungs turning to vapor every time they took a breath. One of the old gents finally spoke up. 'Boy, its cold out here. What do you think?' The other old gent thought for a minute. 'Oh, I don't mind it at all. In fact, it's nice to know I can tell that I'm still breathing."

Both men laughed as the fuel truck driver finished filling the plane's wing tanks. Michael handed the driver his fuel card and the driver took the information from it, handing it back to him. Once the fuel truck was gone, Michael got back into the plane and started it up. He waited for the engines to warm up, then radioed the tower, getting clearance to take off.

Once Michael was in the air, he turned the nose of the plane in the direction of the island. Huge chunks of ice floating in the water below him reflected the moonlight. They looked like cold, blue eyes blinking at him every time they opened and closed their watery eyelids.

Flying between the mainland and the island gave Michael time to think. His thoughts always migrated to his family, friends, his plane, and sometimes, his past. Most of the time he thought about the freedom flying brought. Flying was like breathing to him, and he couldn't do without either one.

He usually kept to his flight plan, but this time

decided against it. In order to run into as little snow as possible, Michael approached the island from the southwest. He found what he thought was County Road Seventeen and began to follow it home. On the way there, the snow and wind hit his plane with a blinding fury from all directions. He couldn't see anything below him or around him.

Michael was concerned, but didn't give in to fear. He'd flown in this same area before in all kinds of weather. He decided to fly by using his instruments. He looked at his altimeter. For some reason it had been sticking lately, giving him false readings. Michael shook his head. One false reading could lead a pilot to think he was flying above tree level, when in reality he would be flying right into them. Michael couldn't take that chance, not in these weather conditions.

He tapped the altimeter; it corrected itself to the right altitude. Satisfied, Michael stuck to his original flight plan. He thought about radioing Cindy, having her and Chris light some flares, placing them near the west end of the runway. He realized that it might be difficult for them, depending on how deep the snow was.

Michael reached into his lunch bucket, pulling out a sandwich that Cindy had made for him, and began to eat it. He glanced at his watch. Only a half hour until he reached where he thought the runway would be. Michael finished the sandwich, wiped his mouth with a paper towel, and took another drink of coffee from his thermos jug. He tapped his altimeter again, nearly dropping the thermos.

Instead of reading two thousand feet, the altimeter suddenly dropped to two hundred feet and kept dropping. Michael quickly increased his air speed and put the plane into a sharp climb. Then, without warning, the world that he knew exploded in a brilliant flash of light!

Back at the house, Cindy was sitting in bed reading a book. She had just dozed off. Suddenly she woke up with a gasp! She was half-soaked in sweat and her heart was beating rapidly. She dropped the book on the floor and got up, looking at the clock on the nightstand. It had been three hours since Michael left. Talking under her breath, she threw on her bathrobe, quickly walking across the hall to Chris's bedroom. She turned on the light, walked over to her daughter's bed, and shook her.

Chris woke up with a start. "What! What do you want? I was sleeping-- why are you so wet?"

Cindy was breathing hard. "Chris, something has happened to your dad. I can feel it!"

Chris took a deep breath and let it out. "Mom, let's stay calm and use our heads. I'll get on the ham radio and see if I can get Dad to answer me. You call Jenny and find out if she or Dan knows anything. Dad said to call Dan if he wasn't back in three hours."

Cindy walked down stairs to the kitchen. The lights were already on when she stepped into the room. Suddenly she stopped and looked at the table in the nook. There sat Grace, wiping tears from her eyes.

"Something's happened to my brother; I know it has." Cindy walked over and held her. "You feel it too, don't you?" Grace nodded. "Yes, and it's the worst feeling I have had in a long time."

Cindy let go of her. "I have to call Jenny and Dan to find out if they've heard anything."

In the meantime, Chris had gotten dressed and gone into the den where the ham radio was located. She turned on the radio, turning the dials to her dad's radio frequency. "Home base to FireDance. Dad, can you read me? Dad! Please answer me!"

Getting no response, she drummed the outside of the radio with her fingers as tears started to form in her eyes. She left the radio on and walked into the kitchen. Cindy had just gotten through talking with Jenny on the phone. She looked at Chris and sighed. "Jenny said that Dan had just called her saying that a high voltage wire had been severed and that he was on his way with the line repair crews to find out why. She said she was coming over here with Maggie and April. Then she hung up."

Cindy turned around and walked over to one of the kitchen windows, looking out at the swirling, drifting snow. A short time later a car horn sounded. Moments later, Jenny opened the back door, walking in with Maggie and April right behind her. Jenny didn't say anything at first. She closed the back door behind her and stood there looking at Cindy and Grace. The look on her face and the flowing tears said more than any words could express.

Just then Melissa came slowly down the back stairs and into the kitchen. She looked at the rest of the women and sighed. "Something's happened to my brother, hasn't it?"

Grace walked over to her and held Melissa in her arms. "I'm afraid it has, sis."

Jenny cleared her throat. "Could one of you take my daughters upstairs and get them settled?"

Chris took Maggie and April by their hands and took them upstairs. As soon as her daughters were out of the room, Jenny spoke, wiping the tears from her eyes. "You know that none of us really knows what's happened to Michael."

Cindy came over, taking her by her shoulders. "Jenny, do you know anything else?"

Jenny gently took Cindy's hands off her shoulders. "All I know is what I told you earlier on the phone. Dan called and said a wire had been severed and that he was on his way with some line repair crews to the area where the break occurred."

Chris had just come down the back stairs, unaware of the conversation going on. "Jenny, are you sure there isn't any more you can tell us?"

Jenny took a deep breath before answering. "I only know what I've told you, Chris. We'll just have to trust God and hope that he is alive and that Dan or someone else will find him before it's too late."

Meanwhile, Michael's plane was disintegrating. He could hear metal tearing and smelled burning aircraft fuel. He felt searing pain and the weird, surrealistic sensation of tumbling in slow motion. He was still strapped to his seat with his arms and legs flopping violently about, like a marionette puppet on strings. Michael screamed out in pain when he hit the ground. Michael slid, still strapped to the plane's seat, across the snow and ice, finally coming to a painful stop. He lay there gasping for breath. Then the stars he was looking up at slowly went blurry. Blackness came. Michael lay quietly in the softly blowing snow, with the burning pieces of his plane silhouetting his still form.

Michael's plane was destroyed. His world of family, friends and flying along with the memories of his past, had come to a crashing halt. All the excuses he had used for not facing the truth had exploded right along with his plane. He had come to the place that God had wanted him to be in for years…the place of total surrender. It was here that God had Michael's heart and soul exactly where he wanted them.

TO BE CONTINUED